PENGUIN CRIME FICTION
Editor: Julian Symons

# MAIGRET AND THE ENIGMATIC LETT

Georges Simenon was born at Liège in Belgium in 1903. At sixteen he began work as a journalist on the *Gazette de Liège*. He has published over 180 novels in his own name, sixty-seven of which belong to the Inspector Maigret series, and his work has been published in thirty-two languages. He has had a great influence upon French cinema, and more than forty of his novels have been filmed.

Simenon's novels are largely psychological. He describes hidden fears, tensions and alliances beneath the surface of life's ordinary routine which suddenly explode into violence and crime. André Gide wrote to him: 'You are living on a false reputation – just like Baudelaire or Chopin. But nothing is more difficult than making the public go back on a too hasty first impression. You are still the slave of your first successes and the reader's idleness would like to put a stop to your triumphs there ... You are much more important than is commonly supposed', and François Mauriac wrote, 'I am afraid I may not have the courage to descend right to the depths of this nightmare which Simenon describes with such unendurable art.'

Simenon has travelled a great deal and once lived on a cutter, making long journeys of exploration round the coasts of Northern Europe. He is married and has four children, and lives near Lausanne in Switzerland. He enjoys riding, fishing and golf.

GEORGES SIMENON

# MAIGRET
# AND THE ENIGMATIC
# LETT

*

TRANSLATED BY
DAPHNE WOODWARD

PENGUIN BOOKS

Penguin Books Ltd, Harmondsworth, Middlesex, England
Penguin Books, 625 Madison Avenue, New York, New York 10022, U.S.A.
Penguin Books Australia Ltd, Ringwood, Victoria, Australia
Penguin Books Canada Ltd, 41 Steelcase Road West, Markham, Ontario, Canada
Penguin Books (N.Z.) Ltd, 182–190 Wairau Road, Auckland 10, New Zealand

—

*Pietr-le-Letton* first published 1931
This translation first published in Penguin Books 1963
Reprinted 1970, 1972, 1974, 1975, 1976

—

Copyright © A. Fayard et Cie, Paris, 1931
Translation copyright © Daphne Woodward, 1963

—

Made and printed in Great Britain
by Cox & Wyman Ltd,
London, Reading and Fakenham
Set in Monotype Garamond

# CHAPTER I

# Age About 32, Height 5 ft 6 ins

*Interpol to Sûreté, Paris:*
 *Xvzust Cracovie vimontra m ghks triv psot uv Pietr-le-Letton
Breme vs tyz btolem.*

Superintendent Maigret, of No. 1 Flying Squad, looked up
from his desk; he had the impression that the iron stove which
stood in the middle of his office, with its thick black pipe
sloping up to the ceiling, was not roaring as loudly as it
should. He pushed aside the paper he had been reading, rose
ponderously to his feet, adjusted the damper and threw in
three shovelfuls of coal.

Then, standing with his back to the stove, he filled a pipe,
and tugged at his shirt collar; it was a low one, but it felt too
tight.

He glanced at his watch; four o'clock. His jacket was hanging from a hook on the door.

Slowly he drifted back to his desk, where he read out the
message in an undertone, decoding it as he went:

*International Criminal Police Commission to Sûreté Générale, Paris:*
 *Police Cracow report Pietr the Lett passed through on way to
Bremen.*

Interpol, the International Criminal Police Commission, at
that time had its headquarters in Vienna, from where, broadly
speaking, it directed the campaign against gangsterism in
Europe, its chief function being to maintain contact between
the police forces in the different countries.

Maigret picked up a telegram, also written in *polcod* – the
secret international language used by police headquarters all
over the world. He read it aloud in 'clear':

*Polizei – Praesidium, Bremen, to Sûreté, Paris:*
 *Pietr the Lett reported making for Amsterdam and Brussels.*

A third telegram, from the Nederlandsche Centrale in Zak Internationale Misdadigers – the Netherlands police head quarters – announced:

*Pietr the Lett left for Paris 11 a.m. by North Star expres coach 5 compartment G.263.*

The final *polcod* telegram came from Brussels, and said:

*Confirm Pietr the Lett passed through Brussels 2 p.m. in Nort Star compartment as reported by Amsterdam.*

On the wall behind Maigret's desk was an enormous map and he now planted himself in front of this, a tall, burly figure hands in pockets and pipe clenched between his teeth.

His eyes travelled from the dot that stood for Cracow to th other dot that indicated the port of Bremen, and from there t Amsterdam and Brussels.

Again he looked at his watch. Twenty past four. The *Nort Star*, doing a steady 66 miles an hour, would now be some where between Saint-Quentin and Compiègne.

No stop at the frontier. No slowing down. In coach 5 compartment G 263, Pietr the Lett was no doubt reading c looking out at the view.

Maigret went to a door and opened it, to reveal a cupboar with an enamel basin and tap. He washed his hands, ran comb through his thick hair – which was dark brown, wit only a few grey threads at the temples – and did his best t straighten a tie he could never persuade to look really neat.

It was November. Dusk was falling. From his office wi dow he could see a stretch of the Seine, the Place Sain Michel, and a floating wash-house, all shrouded in a blue haz through which the gas-lamps twinkled like stars as they l up one by one.

He opened a drawer and glanced through a cable from th International Identification Bureau at Copenhagen:

*Sûreté, Paris*:

*Pietr le Letton 32 169 01512 0224 0255 02732 03116 0323 03243 03325 03415 03522 04115 04144 04147 05221 . . . etc.*

This time he took the trouble to translate aloud, and eve

epeated the words several times, like a schoolboy going over
lesson:

'Apparent age 32 years. Height 5 ft 6½ ins. Nose: bridge
traight, base horizontal, jutting out. Ears: large Original
order, crossed lobe, outward anti-tragus, lower fold
traight; peculiarity – spaces between folds. Long face.
parse light-blond eyebrows. Lower lip prominent, thick,
rooping. Long neck. Eyes: halo around the pupil mid-
ellow, periphery of the iris mid-green. Light blond hair.'

This was a verbal portrait of Pietr, or Piet, the Lett, and to
ne Superintendent it conveyed as much as a photograph. It
escribed the man's general appearance: short, slight, youth-
al, with very fair hair, fair, thin eyebrows, greenish eyes, and
long neck.

It also gave a detailed description of Pietr's ears, so that
Maigret could pick him out in a crowd even if his features
ere disguised.

Maigret took down his jacket, put it on, topped it with a
eavy black overcoat, and placed a bowler hat on his head.

With a parting glance at the stove, which looked about to
low up, he left the office.

At the far end of a long corridor, on the landing that
erved as a waiting-room, he called out:

'Jean, don't forget my fire, will you?' And he began to
escend the stairs. Here a rush of wind took him by surprise,
nd he had to step back into a recess to light his pipe.

he huge glass roof of the Gare du Nord gave no protection
om the gusts of wind that swept the platforms. Several
anes had been dislodged and lay in fragments on the lines.
he lights were dim. People were muffled to the ears.

Beside one ticket-window, a group of travellers stood
eading an ominous announcement:

'Channel gale . . .'

One woman, whose son was crossing to Folkestone, looked
straught and red-eyed. She was pouring out last-minute
structions to him, and making him promise, sheepishly,
ot to go on deck even for a moment.

Maigret stood at the entrance to platform 11, where crowd had gathered to meet the *North Star*. All the big hotels and Cook's, were represented.

Maigret did not move. Some of the others were growing irritable. One young woman, swathed in mink except for he legs in their sheer invisible stockings, was pacing to and fro her stiletto heels clicking on the asphalt.

But he stood motionless, a bulky figure, his impressiv shoulders casting a great shadow. People jostled him, but h swayed no more than a wall would have done.

The yellow dot of the train's light appeared in the distanc Hubbub broke out, the shouts of porters; the passenge began to plod towards the exit.

Two hundred of them had filed past before Maigret spotte among the throng a little man wearing an overcoat with large green check pattern which was as unmistakably Nord in cut as in colour.

The man was not hurrying. He was followed by thre porters, and preceded by the representative of a luxury hot in the Champs-Élysées, obsequiously clearing a path for hin

*Age about 32. Height 5 ft 6½ ins.... Bridge of nose ...*

Maigret, showing no excitement, looked at the ears of th man in green. That settled it.

The man went close by him. One of the three porte bumped the Superintendent's leg with a suitcase.

At that moment one of the train staff came running up an spoke a few hurried words to the ticket-collector, who w₂ standing by a chain that could be used to close the platforn

The chain was thereupon put up. Voices rose in protest.

The man in the green check overcoat had already reache the exit.

The Superintendent was smoking his pipe with short, rapi puffs. He went over to the official who had put up the chain

'Police. What's the matter?'

'A body ... They've just found ...'

'Coach 5?'

'I believe so. ...'

Life in the station was following its normal course. On

platform 11 looked unusual. There were fifty people still there, prevented from leaving. They were growing impatient.

'Let them through,' said Maigret.

'But . . .'

'Let them through. . . .'

He watched this last batch file out. The loudspeaker was announcing the departure of a suburban train. Somewhere, people were running. Beside one of the *North Star* coaches, a little group stood waiting. Three men in railwaymen's uniforms.

The station-master arrived first, pompous but worried. Then a wheeled stretcher was pushed across the main hall of the station, past groups of people who stared after it uncomfortably, especially those about to board trains.

Maigret strode heavily along the platform, still smoking. Coach 1, Coach 2 . . . Coach 5.

This was where the group stood waiting at the door. The stretcher halted. The station-master was listening to the three men, who were all speaking at once.

'Police! . . . Where is he?'

They stared at him with obvious relief. His great bulk thrust into the excited group, making the rest look like nobodies.

'In the toilet. . . .'

Maigret hauled himself up the steps and found the open door of the toilet on his right. A body lay in a heap on the floor, bent double and strangely twisted.

The guard was giving orders from the platform:

'Shunt the coach into a siding. . . . Wait a minute! No. 62. . . . And inform the special Superintendent. . . .'

At first Maigret could only see the back of the man's neck. But he pushed aside the cap, which was perched askew, to reveal the left ear.

'H'm . . . "Crossed lobe, outward anti-tragus . . .",' he muttered.

There were a few drops of blood on the linoleum. He looked around him. The station employees were standing on the platform and the steps. The station-master was still talking.

9

Maigret tipped the man's head back; and his teeth tightened on the stem of his pipe.

If he had not seen the traveller in the green overcoat come out, if he had not seen him walking towards a car, accompanied by an interpreter from the Majestic, he might have doubted his own eyes.

The description fitted. The same small, fair, toothbrush moustache below a narrow-bridged nose. The same fair, thin eyebrows. The same greenish-grey eyes.

In other words, Pietr the Lett!

Maigret could not move in the cramped toilet. A tap no one had thought to turn off was still running and a jet of steam was escaping from a leaky joint in the pipe.

His shins were touching the corpse. He raised its head and shoulders and saw that the jacket and shirt bore scorch-marks across the chest, where a shot had been fired at point-blank range. It had made a big, blackish patch, partly covered by a purple-red bloodstain.

The Superintendent was struck by a small detail. He happened to notice one of the feet. It was lying sideways, twisted like the rest of the body, which had been pushed into a heap so that the door could be closed.

The foot was wearing a very ordinary cheap black shoe: it showed signs of having been re-soled, the heel was worn down on one side, and in the middle of the sole there was a round hole that had gradually worn right through.

The special station Superintendent had arrived, gold-braided and officious; standing on the platform, he fired his questions.

'What's the matter now? ... Violence? ... Suicide? ... Mind you don't touch anything until the Public Prosecutor's men get here! ... Careful! ... It's my responsibility ...'

Maigret had infinite difficulty in getting out of the toilet, entangled as he was in the corpse's legs. With a swift, professional gesture he felt the dead man's pockets, making sure they were empty, absolutely empty.

He stepped down from the train; his pipe had gone out, his

hat was askew, and there was a bloodstain on one of his cuffs.

'Hello, Maigret. You here? . . . What do you think?'

'Nothing! Go ahead. . . .'

'Suicide, surely?'

'If you like. . . . Have you rung the Public Prosecutor's office?'

'The moment I was informed. . . .'

A voice was bellowing through the loudspeaker. A few people had noticed that something unusual was going on; they stood a little way off, watching the empty train and the motionless group clustered outside coach 5.

Maigret left them all to it, walked out of the station and hailed a taxi.

'Majestic Hotel.'

The gale was blowing harder than ever. The streets were swept by whirlwinds that sent people reeling like drunkards. A tile crashed to the pavement. The buses rushed on their way.

The Champs-Élysées looked like a deserted race-track. It was just beginning to rain. The commissionaire outside the Majestic hurried over to the taxi with his huge red umbrella.

'Police! . . . Has someone just arrived off the *North Star*?'

The commissionaire promptly closed his umbrella.

'Yes, that is so.'

'Green overcoat, fair moustache? . . .'

'That's right. Ask reception.'

People were running to escape the downpour. Maigret walked into the hotel just in time to escape a flurry of rain-drops the size of walnuts and as cold as ice.

The impeccably dressed and imperturbable clerks and inter-preters behind the mahogany desk were unaffected by the weather.

'Police! . . . A new arrival – green overcoat, small fair moust —'

'Room 17. They're just taking his luggage up.'

# CHAPTER 2

# The Friend of Millionaires

MAIGRET'S presence at the Majestic inevitably carried a suggestion of hostility. He was a kind of foreign body its organism would not assimilate.

Not that he resembled the policeman dear to caricaturists. He had neither moustache nor heavy boots. His suit was of quite good material and cut; he shaved every morning and had well-kept hands.

But his frame was plebeian – huge and bony. Strong muscles swelled beneath his jacket and soon took the crease out of even a new pair of trousers.

He had a characteristic stance too, which even many of his own colleagues found annoying.

It expressed something more than self-confidence, and yet it was not conceit. He would arrive, massively, on the scene, and from that moment it seemed that everything must shatter against his rock-like form, no matter whether he was moving or standing still with feet planted slightly apart.

His pipe was clamped between his teeth. He was not going to remove it just because he was in the Majestic.

Perhaps, indeed, this vulgar, self-confident manner was assumed deliberately.

With his heavy, black, velvet-collared overcoat he made a conspicuous figure in the brightly-lit hall, where elegant women were coming and going amid whiffs of scent, shrill laughter, and whispers, greeted deferentially by the well-groomed staff.

Maigret paid no attention. He kept aloof from the bustle. The strains of a jazz orchestra drifted up to him from the underground ballroom, then died away, as though stopped by an impenetrable barrier.

As he began to go upstairs the liftman called to him, offering his services. But he did not even turn his head.

On the first floor, someone asked:

'Can I help you?'

The voice did not seem to reach his ears. He looked along the corridors with their endless, sickening expanse of red carpet, and went on and up.

On the second floor, hands in pockets, he began to read the room-numbers on their bronze plates. The door of No. 17 was open. Hotel servants in striped waistcoats were bringing in suitcases.

The new arrival had taken off his overcoat and stood, very slim and elegant in a worsted suit, smoking a cigarette with a cardboard mouthpiece and giving orders.

No. 17 was not a room but a suite – sitting-room, study, bedroom, and bathroom. The door was at a corner where two corridors met, and a big curved sofa stood outside, like a bench at a crossroads.

Maigret sat down on this, directly opposite the open door, stretched out his legs, and unbuttoned his overcoat.

Pietr the Lett noticed him, but went on giving orders, with no sign of surprise or annoyance. When the servants had finished arranging his trunks and suitcases on luggage stands, he came over and shut the door himself, holding it ajar for a second while he scrutinized the Superintendent.

Maigret had time to smoke three pipes and send away two floor-waiters and a chambermaid who came to ask what he was waiting for.

On the stroke of eight, Pietr the Lett emerged from his room, looking slimmer and more clean-cut than ever, in a dinner-jacket whose classic lines bore the mark of Savile Row.

He was bare-headed. His fair, close-cropped hair was beginning to retreat from a slightly receding forehead, and the pink skin showed faintly through it at the top of his head.

He had long, pale hands. On the fourth finger of his left hand he wore a heavy platinum signet ring with a yellow diamond on it.

He was again smoking a Russian cigarette with a cardboard

mouthpiece. He passed close by Maigret, halted as though tempted to speak to him, but then went on, looking thoughtful, towards the lift.

Ten minutes later he appeared in the dining-room and sat down at the table of Mr and Mrs Mortimer-Levingston, which was the centre of attention. Mrs Mortimer-Levingston had ten thousand pounds' worth of pearls round her neck. On the previous day her husband had put one of the biggest French motor-car firms on its feet again – keeping a majority of the shares for himself, of course.

The three of them were chatting gaily. Pietr the Lett talked volubly but quietly, leaning forward a little. He was entirely at ease, unaffected and nonchalant, although he could see Maigret's dark figure in the hall, through the glass partition.

The Superintendent was at the reception desk, asking to look at the visitors' book. He saw without surprise that the guest from Latvia had entered himself as 'Oswald Oppenheim, ship-owner, from Bremen'.

The man undoubtedly had a valid passport and a complete set of papers in that name, as in others.

And he had doubtless met the Mortimer-Levingstons before – in Berlin, Warsaw, London, or New York.

Had he come to Paris solely to meet them and bring off one of the colossal swindles in which he specialized?

His official description – Maigret had the card in his pocket – ran as follows:

'An extremely clever, dangerous man, of uncertain nationality, but Nordic origin. Thought to be Latvian or Estonian. Speaks Russian, French, English, and German fluently.

'Highly educated. Believed to be the leader of a powerful international gang, chiefly concerned in financial swindles.

'This gang has been traced at various times to Paris, Amsterdam (the Van Heuvel case), Berne (the United Shipbuilders case), Warsaw (the Lipmann case), and various other European cities, where its activities have been less positively identified.

'Most of Pietr the Lett's accomplices appear to be from the

14

English-speaking countries. One of those most frequently seen with him, and recognized as the presenter of the forged cheque at the Federal Bank in Berne, was killed while being arrested. He used to pass himself off as Major Howard, of the American Legion, but was discovered to be a former New York bootlegger, known in the United States as Fat Fred.

'Pietr the Lett has been arrested twice. Once at Wiesbaden, for fraudulently obtaining half a million marks from a Munich wholesaler, and once at Madrid for a similar transaction, the victim in that instance being a prominent member of Spanish court society.

'He used the same tactics on both occasions. He had a talk with his victim, and no doubt told him the stolen funds were in a safe place and that his arrest would not lead to their recovery.

'On each occasion the charge was withdrawn and the plaintiff presumably compensated.

'Has never been caught red-handed since.

'Probably has some connexion with the Maronnetti gang (which forges bank-notes and identity papers) and with the "wall-borers" gang in Cologne.'

There was also a persistent rumour in European police circles to the effect that as leader and 'treasurer' of several gangs, Pietr the Lett must have a handsome fortune put by under different names in banks, or even invested in the stock market.

He was now listening with a faint courteous smile to some story that Mrs Mortimer-Levingston was telling him, while his pale fingers plucked magnificent grapes from a large bunch.

'Excuse me, sir; may I have a word with you?'

Maigret was speaking to Mortimer-Levingston in the hall of the Majestic. Pietr the Lett had just gone up to his room, and so had the American's wife.

Mortimer-Levingston did not look at all the athletic Yankee; he was more like a Latin American.

He was tall and slim, with a very small head; his black hair was parted in the middle.

He looked permanently tired. His eyelids were dark and drooping. Indeed, he led an exhausting life, managing some-

15

how to put in regular appearances at Deauville, Miami, the Lido, Paris, Cannes, and Berlin, to join his yacht in some harbour, to complete a deal in a European city, or to be one of the judges at all the biggest boxing matches in New York and California.

He threw Maigret a supercilious glance and murmured without moving his lips:

'Who are you?'

'Superintendent Maigret, No. 1 Flying Squad.'

Mortimer-Levingston frowned almost imperceptibly, and paused with bent head, as though resolved to grant Maigret only a second of his time.

'Are you aware that you have been dining with Pietr the Lett?'

'Is that all you have to say to me?'

Maigret showed no surprise. He had expected some such retort. Putting his pipe between his teeth – for he had condescended to remove it before addressing the millionaire – he grunted:

'That's all!'

He looked rather smug. Mortimer-Levingston walked past him in icy silence, and went into the lift.

It was just after half past nine. The orchestra which had played during dinner now gave way to the jazz band. People were beginning to arrive from outside.

Maigret had not had dinner. He stood where he was, in the middle of the hall, with no sign of impatience. The manager kept glancing at him from a distance, looking worried and cross. Even the most junior employees scowled as they went past, and sometimes deliberately bumped into him.

The Majestic could not stomach him. He stood there obstinately, a great black, motionless patch, contrasting with the gilt, the bright lights, the fashionable crowd with its evening dress, fur coats, perfume, and vivacity.

Mrs Mortimer-Levingston was the first to emerge from the lift. She had changed her dress, and her shoulders were bare beneath a *lamé* cloak lined with ermine.

She seemed astonished that no one was waiting for her, and for a time she strolled about, her high, golden heels tapping rhythmically on the floor.

Suddenly she stopped at the mahogany desk where the clerks and interpreters were waiting, and spoke briefly to them. One of the clerks pressed a red button and picked up the telephone. . . .

Looking surprised, he summoned a page, who ran off to the lift.

Mrs Mortimer-Levingston was becoming visibly uneasy. Through the glass door a streamlined American limousine could be seen, parked just outside.

The page came back and spoke to the clerk, who in his turn said something to Mrs Mortimer-Levingston. She protested. She seemed to be saying:

'That's impossible!'

At this point Maigret walked upstairs, stopped at the door of room 17, and knocked. As he had expected after the scene he had just witnessed, there was no answer.

He opened the door; the sitting-room, he saw, was empty. In the bedroom, Pietr the Lett's dinner-jacket had been flung carelessly on the bed. A wardrobe trunk stood open. Pietr's patent-leather pumps lay on the carpet, far apart.

The manager arrived.

'You here already?' he grunted.

'So he's disappeared, has he?! Mortimer-Levingston as well! Is that it?'

'We mustn't get worked up. They're not in their rooms, but we're sure to find them somewhere about the hotel.'

'How many entrances are there?'

'Three. . . . One on the Champs-Élysées. One into the arcades. And the tradesmen's entrance in the rue de Ponthieu.'

'Is there a watchman there? Send for him.'

The manager took up the telephone. He was furious. He snapped at the switchboard operator who failed to understand him. All the time he glared at Maigret.

'What's the meaning of this?' he inquired, while they

waited for the watchman to arrive from his small glass fronted box beside the tradesmen's entrance.

'Nothing. Or practically nothing, as they say. . . .'

'I hope there hasn't been a . . . a . . .'

The word that stuck in his throat was 'crime', that nightmare of every hotel-keeper in the world, from the humblest lodging-house keeper to the manager of the most luxurious 'palace'.

'We shall soon find out.'

Mrs Mortimer-Levingston appeared.

'Well?' she demanded.

The manager bowed and stammered something unintelligible. Approaching down the corridor was a little old man with an unkempt beard and slovenly clothes, quite out of keeping with the hotel. He was never supposed to come out from the wings, of course; otherwise he too would have worn a smart uniform and got shaved every morning.

'Did you see anyone go out?'

'When?'

'A few minutes ago.'

'One of the kitchen staff, I think. I didn't pay attention. . . A man wearing a cap. . . .'

'Short and fair-haired?' Maigret put in.

'Yes. . . . I think so. . . . I didn't look. . . . He was walking fast. . . .'

'Nobody else?'

'I don't know. . . . I went to the corner of the street to buy an evening paper.'

Mrs Mortimer-Levingston was losing her self-control.

'Good Lord! Is this the way you search for someone?' she snapped, turning to Maigret. 'I'm told you're from the police. My husband may have been killed. . . . What are you waiting for?'

The heavy gaze that he turned on her was a hundred per cent Maigret. Utterly calm. Utterly indifferent. As though he had just heard a fly buzzing. As though he were looking at some completely commonplace object.

She was not used to being looked at like that. She bit her

18

p, blushed scarlet under her make-up, and stamped her foot npatiently.

He went on gazing at her.

Then, driven past bearing, or perhaps not knowing what lse to do, she broke into hysterics.

was nearly midnight when Maigret got back to the Quai es Orfèvres. The storm was in full blast. The trees along the uay were tossing to and fro, and little waves were lapping the ull of the floating wash-house.

The offices of the Judicial Police were almost deserted. ut Jean was still at his post, in the waiting-room that ave on to the corridors with their rows of empty offices.

Loud voices could be heard from the duty room. Here and uere a thread of light showed under a door: a superintendent r inspector was still working on some inquiry. The engine f a police car suddenly snorted in the courtyard.

'Has Torrence got back?' asked Maigret.

'Just this minute.'

'How's my stove going?'

'I had to open the window a crack, it was so hot in your ffice. Water was running down the walls!'

'Order me some beer and sandwiches. Rolls, not sliced :ead, remember!'

He opened a door and shouted:

'Torrence!'

Sergeant Torrence followed him to his office. Before leav- g the Gare du Nord, Maigret had telephoned him to take ɔ the investigation at this end.

The Superintendent was forty-five years old. Torrence was ɪly thirty. But there was already something massive about m that suggested a not quite full-sized replica of Maigret.

They had handled many cases together, never uttering a ɪperfluous word.

The Superintendent took off his overcoat and jacket and ɔsened his tie. Standing with his back to the stove, he ɪused to let the warmth get well into his bones before he ked:

'Well?'

'The Public Prosecutor called an emergency meeting. The Judicial Identification people took some photos, but they found no finger-prints. Except the dead man's, of course. There's no record of those in the files.'

'If I remember rightly, the Department has no file on Pietr?'

'Only his verbal portrait. No prints or measurements.'

'So there's nothing to prove that the corpse is not Pietr?'

'But there's nothing to prove that it is.'

Maigret had picked up his pipe and a tobacco pouch which was empty except for a little brown dust. Automatically, Torrence held out an open packet of tobacco.

Silence. The pipe spluttered faintly. Then they heard footsteps and the clinking of glasses outside the door. Torrence opened it.

The waiter from the Brasserie Dauphine came in with a tray bearing six glasses of beer and four thick sandwiches and put it down on the table.

'Will that be enough?' he inquired, noticing that Maigret was not alone.

'It'll do.'

Still smoking, the Superintendent settled down to eat and drink, after pushing a glass of beer towards his subordinate.

'So?'

'I questioned all the train crew. It turned out there was one man travelling without a ticket. Either the dead man or the murderer! They think he got in at Brussels on the wrong side of the train. It's easier to hide in a Pullman coach than in an ordinary one, because of the big luggage space in each coach. Pietr ordered tea between Brussels and the frontier; he was looking through a batch of English and French newspapers, including several financial ones. Between Maubeuge and Saint Quentin he went out to the toilet. The steward remembered that, because as Pietr went past he said: "Bring me a whisky."'

'And he went back to his seat after a bit?'

'A quarter of an hour later he was sitting with his whisky in front of him. But the steward hadn't seen him come back.'

'Nobody tried to get into the toilet after that?'

'Oh yes. A woman passenger shook the door, but
he handle wouldn't turn. After the train reached Paris, one
f the crew managed to force the door open, and he
ound the mechanism had been put out of action with iron
ilings.'

'No one had seen the second Pietr until then?'

'No. He'd have been noticed, because he was wearing the
ind of shabby clothes that aren't often seen on a Pullman
rain.'

'And the shot?'

'Fired point-blank from a 6-mm. automatic. It burnt the
aan so badly that the doctor says he could have died just from
nat.'

'No signs of a struggle?'

'None at all. His pockets were empty.'

'I know. . . .'

'Oh, sorry! . . . I did find this, in a small inside pocket in
ae waistcoat, which was fastened with a button.'

From his wallet Torrence brought out a transparent
nvelope; a lock of brown hair could be seen inside it.

'Give it here. . . .'

Maigret went on eating and drinking.

'A woman's hair, or a child's?'

'The official pathologist says it's a woman's. I left him a few
airs, and he promised to examine them thoroughly.'

'The post-mortem?'

'All over by ten o'clock. Age about thirty-two. Height
ft 6½ ins. No congenital defects, but one kidney was in a
d way, suggesting that the man was a heavy drinker. The
omach still contained tea and some almost completely
igested food that couldn't be analysed then and there.
hey'll tackle that tomorrow. Once the tests are finished, the
ody will be taken to the Medico-Legal Institute and put on
e.'

Maigret wiped his mouth, returned to his favourite position
front of the stove, and held out a hand into which Torrence,
though by a conditioned reflex, again put his packet of
bacco.

'As for me,' said the Superintendent, 'I saw Pietr, or th
man who's taken his place, settle into the Majestic and hav
dinner with the Mortimer-Levingstons, who seemed to b
expecting him.'

'The multi-millionaires?'

'Yes. After dinner, Pietr went up to his suite. I warned th
American, who went upstairs himself. The three of them mu:
have intended to go out together, because a moment late
Mrs Mortimer-Levingston came down, all dolled up for th
evening. Ten minutes afterwards it was discovered that bot
men had disappeared.

'Pietr had changed from his dinner-jacket into somethin
less conspicuous. He had put on a cap, too, and the porte
took him for one of the kitchen staff. Mortimer-Levingsto
went off just as he was, in evening dress.'

Torrence said nothing. There was a long silence, durin
which they could hear the storm rattling the windows and th
stove roaring.

'The luggage?' asked Torrence at last.

'Been through it. Nothing! Clothes. Linen. Suits. Shirt
Underwear. The complete outfit of a wealthy traveller. Bu
not a single paper. The Mortimer-Levingston woman is cor
vinced her husband has been murdered.'

A church bell rang somewhere. Maigret opened the des
drawer into which, that afternoon, he had thrust the tel
grams about Pietr the Lett.

Then he looked at the map. He drew a line with his finge:
Cracow, Bremen, Amsterdam, Brussels, Paris.

Near Saint-Quentin the finger paused for a moment: a ma
had died.

In Paris the line stopped abruptly. Two men had vanishec
right in the Avenue des Champs-Élysées.

All that remained was some luggage in a hotel suite, an
Mrs Mortimer-Levingston, as devoid of ideas as the ware
robe-trunk in the middle of the Latvian's bedroom.

Maigret's pipe was bubbling so exasperatingly that he too
a bunch of feathers from another drawer and cleaned th

tem; then he opened the stove and threw the dirty feathers
into it.

Four of the beer-glasses were empty, their sides misted
with thick froth. A man came out of one of the neighbouring
offices, locked the door, and walked down the passage.

'One chap who's finished,' remarked Torrence. 'That's
Lucas. He arrested two dope-peddlers this evening, after
some mother's boy gave the show away.'

Maigret poked the stove and stood up again, red-faced.
Absent-mindedly, he picked up the transparent envelope,
took out the hair, and moved it about in the light from his
lamp. Then he went back to the map. The invisible line
marking the Latvian's journey described a definite curve,
almost a semicircle.

Why go from Cracow up to Bremen, before coming down
to Paris?

He was still holding the transparent envelope. 'This had a
photograph in it,' he muttered to himself.

It was, in fact, the kind of envelope into which photo-
graphers put prints for their customers.

But it was of a size not seen nowadays except in villages and
little country towns; what used to be called the 'album format'.

The photo it had once held must have been one of those
pieces of cardboard half the size of a postcard, on which the
actual picture was mounted, printed on a thin slip of glossy
ivory-white paper.

'Is there anyone left in the laboratory?' the Superintendent
asked suddenly.

'I imagine so. They must be working on the train business,
developing their photos.'

There was only one full glass left on the table. Maigret
emptied it at a gulp, and put on his jacket.

'Coming with me? That kind of photo usually has the
photographer's name and address printed on it, incised or
embossed.'

Torrence knew what he meant. They set out, following a
maze of corridors and staircases, up to the attics of the Palais

23

de Justice, and finally reached the Judicial Identificatio
laboratory.

An expert took the envelope, felt it, almost seemed to sn
it. Then he sat down under a powerful lamp and pulled ov
a weird-looking machine mounted on wheels.

The principle is simple enough. If a piece of white paper
left for some time in contact with paper that is covered wit
print or written on in ink, whatever is thus printed or writte
on the second sheet will come off on to the first.

The result is invisible to the naked eye; but the transfer wi
show in a photograph.

Since there was a stove in the laboratory, Maigret inevitab
drifted over to it. He stood there for nearly an hour, smokin
pipe after pipe, while Torrence watched the photograph
moving to and fro.

At last the door of a dark-room opened and a voice a
nounced:

'Got it!'

'Well?'

'The photo was signed *Léon Moutel, art photographer, Qu
des Belges, Fécamp*.'

It took an expert's instinct to read the faint marks on tl
plate, where Torrence, for instance, could see nothing b
vague shadows.

'Want to see the photos of the body?' inquired the expe
affably. 'They're magnificent! Although we were pretty sho
of space in that toilet in the train. Would you believe it, w
had to sling the camera from the ceiling . . .'

'Is that an outside line?' Maigret interposed, pointing t
the telephone.

'Yes. The switchboard operator leaves at nine o'clocl
Then they connect me up with . . .'

The Superintendent rang up the Majestic. One of tl
interpreters took the call.

'Has Mr Mortimer-Levingston got back?'

'I will inquire, sir. Would you kindly tell me who . . .'

'The police.'

'He is not back.'

24

'And neither is Mr Oswald Oppenheim?'

'No.'

'What is Mrs Mortimer-Levingston doing?'

Silence.

'I asked you what Mrs Mortimer-Levingston was doing.'

'She . . . I believe she is in the bar.'

'In other words, she is drunk?'

'Well, she has had a few cocktails. She says she won't go up to her room again until her husband gets back. . . . Is it . . .'

'What?'

'Hello? This is the manager,' said a different voice. 'Are there any developments? Do you think the story will get into the papers?'

Cynically, Maigret rang off. To please the photographer, he glanced at the prints spread out on the driers; they were still damp and shiny.

Meanwhile he was saying to Torrence:

'You move into the Majestic, my lad. And take no notice whatsoever of the manager.'

'What about you, Chief?'

'I shall get back to my office. There's a train to Fécamp at half past five. Not worth going home and waking my wife. By the way – the Brasserie Dauphine will still be open. As you go past, order a glass of beer for me. . . .'

'Only one?' said Torrence, looking innocent.

'Yes, please, old chap. The waiter is bright enough to make it three or four. Tell him to bring a few sandwiches as well.'

One behind the other, they went down an interminable winding staircase.

The black-overalled photographer was left to the pleasure of contemplating the prints he had just made, which he now proceeded to number.

In an icy courtyard, the two policemen separated.

'If you go out of the Majestic for any reason, leave one of our fellows there!' enjoined the Superintendent. 'That's where I shall telephone if I need to.'

He went back to his office, and poked the stove as though he meant to break its bars.

CHAPTER 3

# *The Second Officer of the* Seeteufel

LA BRÉAUTÉ station, where Superintendent Maigret left the
main-line train from Paris to Le Havre at half past seven in
the morning, gave him a foretaste of Fécamp.

An ill-lit refreshment room with grimy walls, and a buffet
on which a few biscuits were mouldering and three bananas
and five oranges were doing their best to form a pyramid.

The storm felt more violent here. The rain was coming
down in buckets. To get from one platform to another meant
wading up to one's knees in mud.

A repulsive little train, assembled from obsolete rolling-
stock. Farms visible in faint outline in the pale daybreak,
almost concealed by the streams of falling rain.

Fécamp! A dense reek of salt cod and herring. Stacks of
barrels. Masts beyond the railway engines. A foghorn moan-
ing somewhere.

'The Quai des Belges?'

Straight ahead. He only had to go on walking through the
slimy puddles where fish scales glittered and fish offal lay
rotting.

The art photographer was a shopkeeper and newsagent as
well. He sold sou'westers, red sailcloth jerkins, seamen's
jerseys, hempen rope, and New Year cards.

He was a puny, washed-out creature, who called his wife to
the rescue as soon as the word 'police' was uttered. She was a
handsome Norman type, who looked Maigret straight in the
eye and almost seemed to be making advances to him.

'Could you tell me what photograph used to be in this
envelope?'

It took a long time. Maigret had to prise the words out of
the photographer one by one, doing his thinking for him.

To begin with, the photograph must be at least eight years

26

old, for he had given up making that format eight years ago, when he bought a new camera which took postcard-size photographs.

Who might have been photographed eight years ago? It took Monsieur Moutel a quarter of an hour to remember that he kept an album with a copy of every photograph produced in his studio.

His wife went to fetch it. Sailors went in and out. Children came to buy a pennyworth of sweets. Outside, the rigging creaked on the boats and the sea tumbled the pebbles against the breakwater.

Maigret, turning the pages of the album, gave a further detail:

'A young woman with very fine brown hair . . .'

That was enough.

'Madame Swaan!' exclaimed the photographer.

And he found the photo at once. It was the only time he had had a presentable sitter.

She was a pretty woman. She looked about twenty years old. The photo fitted the envelope perfectly.

'Who is she?'

'She still lives at Fécamp. But now she has a villa on the cliff, five minutes', walk from the Casino.'

'Married?'

'She wasn't in those days. She was the receptionist at the Railway Hotel.'

'Opposite the station, of course?'

'Yes, you must have seen it as you went by. She was an orphan, from a village near here. . . . Les Loges – do you know it? That's how she met a guest who was staying at the hotel – a foreigner. They got married. And now she lives in her villa, with her two children and a maid. . . .'

'Doesn't Monsieur Swaan live at Fécamp?'

There was a silence. The photographer and his wife exchanged glances. She spoke first.

'As you're from the police, we'd better tell you everything, hadn't we? In any case you'd find out. . . . It's nothing but rumours. . . . Monsieur Swaan is hardly ever at Fécamp. When

27

he does come, he only stays a few days. . . . Sometimes h
doesn't even stay the night. . . . The first time he arrived wa
soon after the war. The Newfoundland Fisheries were bein
restarted, after a five-year stoppage. . . .

'The story was that he wanted to look into the question an
invest money in the businesses that were being launched.

'He said he was a Norwegian. His first name is Olaf. Th
herring fishers, who sometimes go as far as Norway, say a lo
of people there have that name. . . .

'All the same, there was a rumour that he was really
German spy.

'So when he got married, people wouldn't have anything t
do with his wife. . . .

'Then it turned out he was a sailor, second officer of
German merchant vessel, and that was why he came s
seldom. . . .

'In the end the gossip died down, but people like us stil
don't trust him. . . .'

'You say they have children?'

'Two. A little girl of three and a baby a few months old.'

Maigret detached the picture from the album and asked th
way to the villa. It was still rather too early to call there.

For two hours he waited in a harbour café, listening to th
fishermen discussing the herring season, which was in fu
swing. Five black trawlers were lying alongside the quay
Fish were being unloaded by the barrel and the air stank c
them, in spite of the gale.

To get to the villa he went along the deserted promenade an
round the closed casino, its walls still adorned with las
summer's posters.

Finally he came to a steep path climbing up from the foot c
the cliff. At intervals he passed the iron gate of a villa.

The one he was looking for turned out to be a comfortabl
looking medium-sized red brick house. The garden, with i
white gravel paths, was obviously well tended in the summ
months, and there must be a fine view from the windows.

He rang the bell. A Great Dane came and sniffed at hi
through the gate – without barking, but looking all the fierc

'or that. Maigret rang again, and a maid appeared. After
hutting the dog into its kennel, she asked:
'What is it?'
She spoke with a local accent.
'I would like to see Monsieur Swaan, please.'
She seemed to hesitate.
'I don't know if Monsieur is at home. . . . I'll ask. . . .'
She had not opened the gate. It was still raining in torrents.
Maigret was drenched.
He watched the servant go up the steps into the house.
Then a curtain stirred at one of the windows. After a while the
girl came back.
'Monsieur will not be home for several weeks. He's at
Bremen. . . .'
'In that case I would like to speak to Madame Swaan.'
Again she hesitated, but finally opened the gate.
'Madame is not dressed yet. You will have to wait. . . .'
Dripping with water, he was shown into a trim living-room
with white-curtained windows and a gleaming parquet floor.
The furniture was new, precisely the same as in any other
middle-class home – good-quality stuff, in the style called
'modern' in 1900.
Light oak. Flowers in an 'artistic' stone jar in the middle of
the table. Broderie anglaise table-mats.
But on a small side-table stood a magnificent embossed
silver samovar, worth more than all the rest of the furniture
put together.
There were sounds from somewhere on the first floor.
Somewhere else, in one of the downstairs rooms, a baby was
crying and another voice was speaking softly in a monotone,
as though trying to comfort it.
At last, light footsteps came along the corridor. The door
opened and Superintendent Maigret found himself confronted
by a young woman who had dressed hurriedly in order to
receive him.
She was of medium height, rather on the plump side, with a
pretty, serious face that now wore an expression of vague
uneasiness.

29

Nevertheless, she smiled as she said:

'Why didn't you sit down?'

Water was trickling from Maigret's overcoat, his trousers and his shoes and forming little pools on the polished floor.

In such a state he could not possibly have sat down in one of the pale green velvet armchairs in that room.

'You are Madame Swaan, are you not?'

'Yes, Monsieur. . . .'

She looked inquiringly at him.

'Forgive me for disturbing you. It is just a formality. . . . I belong to the foreign supervisory department of the police force. We are making a census at the moment. . . .'

She said nothing. Her uneasiness seemed neither to increase nor to diminish.

'I believe Monsieur Swaan is of Swedish nationality?'

'No, Norwegian. . . . But to the French it is the same thing. . . . Even I, at first . . .'

'He is an officer in the merchant service?'

'Second officer of the *Seeteufel* of Bremen . . .'

'That's it. . . . So he works for a German company?'

Her colour deepened.

'The owners are German, yes. . . . At least on paper. . . .'

'Which means to say?'

'I don't see why I shouldn't tell you. . . . I expect you know that since the war there has been a lot of unemployment among merchant seamen. In this town alone you'll hear of several captains who could not get a boat and have had to sign on as second or third officers. Others have joined the Newfoundland or North Sea fishing fleets.'

She spoke rather hurriedly, but her voice was soft and steady.

'My husband didn't want to sign on for the Pacific, where there are more opportunities, because he would have been away from Europe for two years at a time. Soon after we were married, some Americans fitted out the *Seeteufel* in the name of a German ship-owner. And the reason Olaf came to Fécamp in the first place was to find out if there were any other schooners for sale here.

30

'Now you see what I mean. . . . They were to smuggle drink to the United States. . . .

'Several big companies were floated, with American money. Some are registered in France, others in Holland or Germany.

'It's for one of these that my husband is really working. The Seeteufel is on what's called the "Rum Avenue run".

'So he has no connexion with Germany. . . .'

'Is he at sea just now?' asked Maigret, his eyes still on the pretty face – which had a frank, even at times a touching expression.

'I don't think so. You must realize that the ship doesn't sail regularly as a liner. But I always try to calculate the Seeteufel's position as exactly as I can. At this moment she should be at Bremen, or very nearly.'

'Have you ever been to Norway?'

'Never! I've hardly ever left Normandy. Just two or three times, for short visits to Paris.'

'With your husband?'

'Yes. On our honeymoon, for one thing.'

'He's a fair-skinned man, isn't he?'

'Yes. . . . Why do you ask?'

'With a small, fair moustache, clipped short?'

'Yes . . . in fact I can show you a photograph of him.'

She opened a door and went out. Maigret heard her moving about in the next room.

She was away longer than seemed reasonable. And from other parts of the house came the sounds of doors opening and shutting and of unaccountable footsteps coming and going.

At last she reappeared, looking rather disturbed and hesitant.

'I'm sorry,' she said. 'I can't put my hand on that photograph. With children about, the house is always in a muddle. . . .'

'One more question. . . . To how many people have you given a copy of this photo?'

He showed her the proof that the photographer had given him. Madame Swaan blushed scarlet.

'I don't understand . . .' she faltered.

'Your husband has a copy of it, no doubt?'

'Yes. . . . We were engaged when . . .'

'No other man has a copy?'

She was on the verge of tears. Her lips trembled, betrayin
her bewilderment.

'No. . . .'

'Thank you, Madame. . . .'

As he was leaving, a little girl slipped out into the hal
Maigret had no need to inspect her features closely. She wa
the living image of Pietr the Lett!

'Olga!' her mother scolded, pushing the child towards
half-open door.

The Superintendent found himself outside again, in the rai
and the blustering wind.

'Good-bye, Madame. . . .'

He caught a last glimpse of her as the door closed, and h
felt he was leaving her in distress, after taking her by surpris
in her cosy house.

And there were other subtle, indefinable signs of anxiet
in the young mother's eyes as she closed the door behind hin

## CHAPTER 4

# *The Drunken Russian*

THERE are things that one doesn't boast about, which would sound comic if described in words, yet which call for a certain degree of heroism.

Maigret had had no sleep. From half past five to eight o'clock that morning he had been jolting along in draughty trains.

Ever since La Bréauté he had been drenched to the skin. Now, dirty water squelched out of his shoes at every step, his bowler hat was shapeless, his coat and jacket wringing wet.

The wind was hurling the rain against him so that it felt like repeated body-blows. The lane was deserted. It was no more than a steep path between garden walls, with a stream rushing down the middle.

He stood there for quite a time. Even his pipe, in his pocket, was wet. There was nowhere close to the house where he could hide. The best he could do was to flatten himself against a wall and wait.

Anyone who went by would see him and look round. He might have to wait there for hours and hours. He had no definite proof that there was a man in the house. And if there were, would he feel inclined to go out?

All the same, Maigret, glumly stuffing tobacco into his wet pipe, pressed back as far as possible into a slight bend in the wall.

This was no job for an officer of the Judicial Police. It was beginner's stuff. He had kept watch like this a hundred times, when he was between twenty-two and thirty years old.

He had a terrible job striking a match. The sandpaper was peeling off the box. If one of the wooden chips had not miraculously caught light at last, he would perhaps have gone away.

B

From where he stood, he could see nothing but a low wall and the green-painted gate of the villa. His feet were in a patch of brambles. There was a cold wind blowing down his neck.

Fécamp lay below, but he could not see it. He could only hear the crashing waves, with now and then the wail of a foghorn or the sound of a passing car.

He had been mounting guard for half an hour when a woman who looked like a cook came up the path, carrying a basket of provisions. She did not see Maigret till she was actually passing him. His huge form, standing motionless against a wall in that wind-swept lane, frightened her so badly that she began to run.

She probably worked in one of the houses higher up the hill. A few minutes later a man appeared at the bend in the lane; a woman joined him, then the pair of them went back indoors.

The situation was ridiculous. The Superintendent knew there was not one chance in ten that his vigil would lead to any result.

But he stuck to it, because of a vague impression; he could not even have called it a presentiment. It was more like a private theory, which he had never even worked out but which just stuck nebulously at the back of his mind; he called it the theory of the chink.

Every criminal, every gangster, is a human being. But he is first and foremost a gambler, an adversary; that is how the police are inclined to regard him, and as such they usually try to tackle him.

When a crime or felony is committed, it is dealt with on the strength of various more or less impersonal data. It is a problem with one – or more – unknown factors, to be solved, if possible, in the light of reason.

Maigret used the same procedure as anyone else. And like everyone else he employed the wonderful techniques devised by Bertillon, Reiss, Locard, and others, which have turned police work into a science.

But above all he sought for, waited for, and pounced on

34

*the chink*. In other words, the moment when the human being showed through the gambler.

At the Majestic he had been confronted by the gambler. Here, he sensed a difference. This quiet, neat villa was not one of the pawns in the game that Pietr the Lett was playing. That young woman, and the children Maigret had glimpsed and heard, belonged to an entirely different material and moral universe.

That was why he waited – though crossly, for he was much too fond of his big iron stove and his office, with the frothing beer-glasses on the table, to be anything but miserable in this clammy storm.

He had taken up his position shortly after ten o'clock. It was half past twelve by the time footsteps crunched on the gravel; the gate was opened by a quick, deft hand, and a figure appeared ten yards away.

The lie of the land allowed Maigret no retreat. So he stayed where he was, motionless, or rather, inert, planted firmly on legs to which his rain-soaked trousers clung in large, smooth patches.

The man who came out of the villa was wearing a shabby, belted trench-coat, its threadbare collar turned up. There was a grey cap on his head.

Thus clad, he looked very young. He set off down the hill, with his hands in his pockets and his hunched shoulders shivering because of the sudden change of temperature.

He had to pass within a yard of the Superintendent. That was the moment he chose to slacken his pace, take a packet of cigarettes from his pocket, and light one.

As though he were deliberately showing his face in the brightest possible light and letting the police officer have a good look at it!

Maigret allowed him to go a few steps farther, and then, frowning, set off in pursuit. His pipe had gone out. Every inch of his person expressed ill humour, coupled with an impatient determination to understand.

For the man in the trench-coat was and yet was not like the Lett. The same height – about five foot six. The same age, at a pinch, though in those clothes he looked more like twenty-six than thirty-two.

There was no reason why he should not be the subject of the 'verbal portrait' that Maigret knew by heart and of which he had a copy in his pocket.

And yet this was a different man! His eyes, for instance, had a softer, more pensive expression. They were a lighter grey, as though watered down by the rain.

He had no small, fair, toothbrush moustache. But that was not the only change in his appearance.

Other points occurred to Maigret. He was not dressed at all in the style of a merchant navy officer. Or even in a way befitting the villa, with its atmosphere of middle-class comfort.

His shoes were shabby, down at heel. He had turned up his trousers because of the mud, and the Superintendent saw that he was wearing grey cotton socks, faded and clumsily darned.

The trench-coat was all spotted and stained. The whole effect suggested a type well known to Maigret – the European vagrant, nearly always from Eastern Europe, who haunts the lowest type of Paris lodging-house, sometimes sleeps in railway stations, seldom ventures into the provinces, and then travels third-class or ticketless on the steps of trains or in goods trucks.

A few minutes later he had proof of this. Fécamp had no real brothels; but behind the harbour there were two or three sordid dives more popular with stokers than with fishermen.

Ten yards away from these establishments stood a respectable, clean, well-lit café.

But the man in the trench-coat went straight past this, stepped unhesitatingly into the most squalid of the dives, and propped his elbows on the bar with a gesture that spoke for itself.

It was a familiar gesture, casual, vulgar. Even had he wanted to, Maigret could not have imitated it.

He went in, too. The man had ordered an absinthe substitute, and stood without a word, vacant-eyed, showing no interest in Maigret, who stood beside him.

Beneath the man's unbuttoned coat collar, the Superintendent saw a grubby shirt: another thing that cannot be faked! That shirt, and that collar, reduced to a mere string, had been worn for days and nights, more likely for weeks on end. The wearer had slept in them, heaven knows where. He had sweated in them, been rained on in them.

The suit had a certain style about it, but it bore the same marks, spoke of the same filthy, vagabond life.

'Same again.'

The man's glass was empty. The café-keeper refilled it and poured out a dram of spirits for Maigret.

'So here you are again, eh?'

The man made no reply; he drank his second apéritif at one gulp, like the first, and pushed his glass back across the counter, indicating that he wanted another refill.

'Will you have something to eat? I've got some soused herring. . . .'

Maigret had manoeuvred himself across to a little stove and now stood with his back to it, as shiny as a wet umbrella. The patron was not to be discouraged. With a wink at the Superintendent, he spoke to the customer in the trench-coat again.

'By the way, there was a fellow-countryman of yours in here last week. A Russian from Archangel. He came off a Swedish three-master that had to put in here because of the storm. He hadn't much time to get tight, I can tell you! They had a hell of a lot of work. . . . Sails torn, two masts gone – the devil's own mess.'

The other man, now at his fourth absinthe, was drinking with concentration. The *patron* filled his glass the moment it was empty, each time with a conspiratorial wink at Maigret.

'As for Captain Swaan, he's not been back since the last time I saw you. . . .'

Maigret started. The man in the trench-coat, who had just emptied his fifth glass of neat spirits, lurched across to the stove, knocking into the Superintendent, and held out his hands to warm them.

'I'll have a herring after all,' he said.

He spoke with a fairly strong accent – Russian, so far as Maigret could judge.

There they were, side by side, practically rubbing shoulders. Several times the man passed his hand over his face, and his eyes were becoming dimmer and dimmer.

'Where's my glass?' he demanded impatiently.

It had to be put into his hand. As he drank, he stared hard at Maigret and screwed up his face in disgust.

There was no mistaking his expression! And as though to make his sentiments even clearer, he flung his glass on the floor, clutched the back of a chair to steady himself, and muttered something in a foreign language.

The *patron*, slightly perturbed, invented some reason for passing close to Maigret and said in what was meant to be a whisper, but loud enough for not a word to escape the Russian:

'Take no notice! He's always like that. . . .'

The man laughed, a smothered, drunken laugh. He subsided on to the chair, dropped his head into his hands, and sat motionless until a plate of soused herring was thrust on to the table between his elbows.

The café-keeper shook him by the shoulder.

'Eat! It'll do you good. . . .'

The man laughed again, with a bitter coughing sound. He turned his head, looking for Maigret, stared impudently at him and pushed the plate of herring off the table.

'Wan'a drink!'

The *patron* raised his hands to heaven and growled apologetically:

'Oh, these Russians!'

And he swivelled a finger round on his forehead.

Maigret had pushed back his bowler hat. Grey steam was rising from his clothes. He had only reached his second dram.

'I'll have a herring,' he said.

He was eating it with a piece of bread when the Russian rose shakily to his feet, looked round as though not knowing hat to do next, and laughed jeeringly, for the third time, as is eyes fell on Maigret.

Then he reeled over to the bar, took a glass off the shelf, and fted a bottle out of the pewter basin where it was standing in old water.

He helped himself without looking to see what it was, icking his tongue as he drank.

Finally he produced a hundred-franc note from his pocket. 'That enough, clot?' he demanded, and tossed the note to the air. The publican had to fish it out of the sink.

The Russian tugged at the door handle, but the door would ot open. There was nearly a row, because the café-keeper ied to help the man, who kept pushing him away with his bow.

At last the trench-coat vanished into the mist and rain, oing along the quay towards the station.

'Queer fellow!' sighed the publican to Maigret, who was aying his bill.

'Does he come here often?'

'Every now and then. ... He once spent the night on the inch where you were sitting. ... He's Russian. So I was told y some Russian sailors that came in one day when he was ire. It seems he's an educated man. Did you notice his ands?'

'Don't you think he's very like Captain Swaan?'

'Oh, you know him? Yes, indeed! Not so much that one ould take one for the other, but all the same ... For a long me I thought they were brothers. ...'

he putty-coloured figure disappeared round a corner. Iaigret began to hurry.

He caught up with the Russian just as he was entering the ird-class waiting-room at the station, where he slumped on a bench and put his head between his hands again.

An hour later they were seated in the same compartment, gether with a cattle-dealer from Yvetot, who proceeded to ll Maigret funny stories in the Normandy patois, nudging

39

him with his elbow now and then to call his attention to their neighbour.

The Russian slid down imperceptibly until he was huddled on the seat with his pallid face sunk on his chest and his mouth open; his breath reeked of alcohol.

CHAPTER 5

## At the Roi de Sicile

THE Russian woke at La Brêauté and did not go to sleep again. Indeed, the Havre–Paris express was so full that Maigret and his companion had to stand in the corridor, outside the doors of two neighbouring compartments, looking out at the blurred scenery which rushed past the windows and was gradually swallowed up by the falling night.

The man in the trench-coat took not the slightest notice of the police officer. Nor did he try to escape from him in the crowd at Saint-Lazare station.

On the contrary, he went slowly down the wide staircase, noticed that his packet of cigarettes was soaking wet, bought another at the tobacconist's shop in the station, almost stopped at the refreshment bar. Changing his mind, he set out along the pavement, dragging his feet – a depressing figure, for he seemed utterly indifferent to his surroundings, so listless as to be incapable of any response.

It is a long walk from Saint-Lazare to the Hôtel de Ville, right through the centre of the city, and between six and seven in the evening crowds are pouring out on to the pavements and cars rush along the streets in a steady flow, like blood circulating through the human body.

The narrow-shouldered Russian, in his tightly-belted raincoat with its mud stains and grease spots, and his down-at-heel shoes, stumbled through the bustle, under the lights, getting jostled and pushed, never pausing or looking behind him.

He took the shortest route, down the rue du 4 Septembre and through Les Halles; he obviously knew the way well.

Reaching the Jewish quarter, centred on its nucleus, the rue des Rosiers, he walked past shops with Yiddish inscriptions,

41

kosher butchers, and bakeries that displayed unleavened bread.

At the corner of an alley as long and dark as a tunnel, a woman tried to take his arm; but she released him, looking scared, without his having uttered a word.

At last he came to the rue du Roi de Sicile, a crooked street fringed with blind alleys, narrow passages, and crowded courtyards – still half Jewish, but already half a Polish colony – and here, after two hundred yards, he turned into the lobby of a hotel.

The name of the place, displayed in ceramic letters, was Au Roi de Sicile.

Below it were inscriptions in Hebrew, Polish, and other incomprehensible languages, probably including Russian.

Next door was a yawning gap with the remains of a house that had been shored up by beams.

It was still raining, but this backwater was sheltered from the wind.

Maigret heard the sound of a window being slammed on the third floor of the hotel. Showing no more hesitation than the Russian, he went in.

No door to the lobby: the stairs went straight up. On the first floor was a kind of glass-fronted box, where a Jewish family sat eating.

The Superintendent knocked. Instead of opening the door, someone pushed up a little window. A sour smell came out. The Jew wore a black skull-cap. His fat wife went on eating.

'What do you want?'

'Police! What is the name of the resident who has just come in?'

The man muttered something in his own language, produced a dog-eared ledger from a drawer, and pushed it through the window without a word.

At the same moment Maigret sensed that he was being watched from the dark staircase. Turning his head sharply, he saw an eye glittering about ten steps above him.

'Which room?'

'Thirty-two.'

He turned the pages of the register, and read:

'Fédor Yurovich, aged 28, born at Vilna, labourer, and Anna Gorskin, aged 25, born at Odessa, no occupation.'

The Jew had returned to his seat and his meal, like a man with a clear conscience. Maigret drummed on the pane, and he got up again, slowly and reluctantly.

'How long has he been living here?'

'About three years.'

'And Anna Gorskin?'

'She was here before him. . . . Four and a half years, maybe.'

'What do they live on?'

'You saw him. He's a working man.'

'Come off it!' Maigret exclaimed, in a tone that effectively changed the other man's attitude.

'The rest is no business of mine, is it?' he remarked, his manner more ingratiating. 'He pays regularly. He comes and goes; it's not my job to trail him. . . .'

'Does he have visitors?'

'Now and then. . . . I've got more than sixty residents, and I can't keep an eye on all of them. So long as they don't get up to any mischief! . . . Anyhow, if you're from the police, you must know the house. My books have always been in order. Sergeant Vermouillet will tell you so. He's the one who calls here every week. . . .'

Maigret suddenly wheeled round and called out:

'Come down, Anna Gorskin!'

There was a faint sound on the stairs, and then came footsteps. Finally, a woman emerged into the ray of light.

She looked older than her registered age of 25. A question of race, no doubt. Like many Jewish women of her age, she had put on weight, but without losing all trace of beauty. She had wonderful eyes, the whites very clear and brilliant and the pupils velvety black.

But in other respects she displayed a slovenliness which

spoilt the impression. Her black hair was greasy and unkempt, hanging down to her shoulders in thick strands. She wore a shabby dressing-gown, which hung open, showing her underwear. Her stockings were rolled down below podgy knees.

'What were you doing on the stairs?'

'I live here. . . .'

Maigret realized at once what kind of woman he had to deal with. Passionate and shameless, she was spoiling for a fight. At the slightest excuse she would start a scene, rouse the whole house with her screams, and probably make the wildest accusations.

Perhaps she knew her position was unassailable. At any rate she was staring defiantly at the enemy.

'You'd do better to keep an eye on your boy-friend.'

'That's my business.'

The hotel-keeper stood at his little window, turning his head from left to right and back again with a grieved reproachful expression; but there was amusement in his eyes.

'When did Fédor leave you?'

'Last night. . . . At eleven o'clock.'

She was lying, obviously. But a head-on clash with her would do no good. Unless he went the whole hog and took her off to the station.

'Where does he work?'

'Where he pleases.'

Her breasts were quivering under the half-open dressing-gown. Her lip curled disdainfully.

'What do the police want with Fédor?'

Maigret thought it better to lower his voice as he said:

'Get along upstairs. . . .'

'When I choose! I don't take orders from you.'

To retort would merely provoke some ridiculous incident which might prejudice his investigation.

Maigret closed the ledger and handed it back to the hotel-keeper.

'It's in order, isn't it?' said the latter, who had signed to the young woman to keep quiet.

But she stayed where she was, hands on hips, half of her

44

body visible in the light from the lodge, the other half in darkness.

The Superintendent looked at her again. She met his eye and could not resist muttering:

'Oh, I'm not afraid of you!'

He shrugged his shoulders and went away downstairs, brushing against the whitewashed wall on either side.

In the passage he ran into two collarless Poles, who looked away when they saw him coming.

The street was wet, the cobbles gleaming.

In every corner, in every little patch of darkness, up the blind alleys and the corridors, one could sense the presence of a swarming mass of humanity, a sly, shameful life. Shadows slunk along the walls. The shops were selling goods unknown to French people even by name.

Less than a hundred yards away were the rue de Rivoli and the rue Saint-Antoine – wide and well-lit, with their buses, their shops, and their police.

Maigret stopped a flap-eared urchin who was running past, by grabbing his shoulder, and said:

'Go and fetch me a policeman from the Place Saint-Paul.'

But the child stared at him, completely baffled, and stammered something unintelligible. He did not know a word of French!

The Superintendent's eye fell on a ragged figure.

'Here's five francs,' he said. 'Take this note to the cop in the Place Saint-Paul.'

The tramp understood. Ten minutes later a uniformed policeman appeared.

'Ring up the Judicial Police and tell them to send me an inspector at once. Dufour, if possible.'

He paced up and down for a good half-hour after that. People went into the hotel. Others came out. But the second window from the left on the third floor was still lit up.

Anna Gorskin appeared in the doorway. She had put on a greenish coat over her dressing-gown. Her head was bare, and in spite of the rain her feet were shod in red satin mules.

She splashed across the street. Maigret drew back into the shadows. She went into a shop, came out again after a few minutes with her arms full of little white parcels, topped by two bottles, and disappeared back into the hotel.

Inspector Dufour arrived at last. He was a man of 35 who spoke three languages fairly fluently; this made him useful, despite his passion for complicating even the simplest matters.

He would work up an ordinary burglary or a smash-and-grab case into a mysterious drama and then lose his head in the middle of it.

But being uncommonly tenacious, he was the very man for a specific assignment, such as watching a house or trailing somebody.

Maigret gave him a description of Fédor Yurovich and his mistress.

'I'll send you one of the other chaps. If either of those two comes out, you follow him or her; but someone must stay here on guard. Understand?'

'This is still the *North Star* business? The Mafia was responsible for that, wasn't it?'

The Superintendent thought it best to go away. A quarter of an hour later he was back at the Quai des Orfèvres, had sent another detective to join Dufour, and was bending over his stove and cursing Jean, who had not managed to get it red hot.

His wet overcoat, on its hanger, was quite stiff and still kept the shape of his shoulders.

'Did my wife ring up?'

'Yes, this morning. We told her you were off on a job.'

She was accustomed to that. He knew that when he got home she would just kiss him, move her saucepans about on the stove, and fill a plate with savoury stew. At most she might venture – once he had sat down to table and she was watching him with her chin propped on her hands – to inquire :

'Everything all right?'

Whether at midday or at five in the afternoon, he would find a meal ready just the same.

'Torrence?' he asked Jean.

'He telephoned at seven o'clock this morning.'

'From the Majestic?'

'I don't know. He asked if you had left.'

'And then?'

'He rang up again in the afternoon, at ten past five. He asked me to tell you he was waiting for you.'

Maigret had had nothing to eat all day except a herring. He stood for a few minutes in front of his stove, which was beginning to roar, for he had an inimitable gift for coaxing the most sullen coals into flame.

At last he strode heavily to the cupboard, which concealed a wash-basin, a towel, a mirror, and a suitcase. He carried the suitcase into the middle of the room, undressed, put on dry clothes and a clean shirt, and ran hesitant fingers across his unshaven chin.

'Oh, never mind. . . .'

He threw a longing glance at the stove which was now burning so well, placed two chairs close to it, and draped his wet garments carefully over them. The last of the previous night's sandwiches was still lying on his desk and he wolfed it down, standing ready to leave. But there was no beer, and his throat felt rather dry.

'If anything turns up for me, I'm at the Majestic,' he said to Jean. 'Tell them to telephone me there.'

And at last he settled back into a taxi.

# CHAPTER 6

# Third Interval

MAIGRET found that his colleague Torrence was not in the hall, but in a room on the first floor, where an excellent dinner was being served. The Sergeant gave the ghost of a wink.

'It's the manager!' he explained. 'He'd rather have me up here than downstairs. He almost implored me to accept this room and the delicious meals he's been sending up to me.'

Speaking softly, he pointed to a door.

'The Mortimer-Levingstons are through there. . . .'

'So Mortimer-Levingston got back?'

'About six o'clock this morning – wet, muddy, and furious, with his clothes all covered in chalk, or whitewash.'

'What did he say?'

'Nothing. He tried to get up to his room without being seen. But they told him his wife was waiting for him in the bar. And she was! She had finally invited a Brazilian couple to drink with her. The bar stayed open just for them. She was dreadfully tight.'

'So then?'

'He turned pale. His lips curled. He nodded curtly to the Brazilians and then took hold of his wife by the waist and dragged her away without a word. I think she must have slept until four in the afternoon. There wasn't a sound from their suite before that. Then I heard whispers. Mortimer-Levingston rang downstairs for the newspapers.'

'They said nothing about the business, I hope?'

'Nothing. They obeyed instructions. Just a short paragraph to say a body's been found in the *North Star* and the police think it's suicide.'

'What happened next?'

'The waiter brought them up some *citron pressé*. At six o'clock Mortimer-Levingston came down to the hall, looking worried; he passed close by me two or three times. He sent off cables in cipher to his New York bank and to his secretary, who's been in London for the last few days.'

'Is that all?'

'At the moment they're just finishing dinner. Oysters, roast chicken, and salad. I get told about everything that goes on. The manager is so delighted to have shut me up here that he can't do too much for me. For instance, he came up just now to tell me that the Mortimer-Levingstons have seats for the play at the Gymnase – a four-act thing called *L'Épopée*. I forget who it's by. . . .'

'What about Pietr's rooms?'

'Nothing doing. Nobody has been in there. I locked the door and stuffed a little ball of wax into the lock, so no one can get in without my finding out. . . .'

Maigret had picked up a leg of chicken and was gnawing it unashamedly, while looking round in vain for a stove. In the end he sat down on the radiator and inquired:

'Anything to drink?'

Torrence poured him out a glass of excellent white Mâcon, and he swallowed it with relish. At that moment there was a light knock on the door and a servant came in, looking furtive.

'The manager sent me to tell you that Mr and Mrs Mortimer-Levingston have ordered their car.'

Maigret looked at the table, still loaded with food; his face wore the same mournful expression with which he had gazed at his office stove.

'I'll go,' he said regretfully. 'You stay here.'

He tidied himself up a little in front of the mirror, wiped his mouth and chin. A moment later he was waiting in a taxi for the Mortimer-Levingstons to come out to their car.

They soon appeared, he in a black overcoat which hid his evening dress, she swathed in furs as on the previous night.

She must be tired, for her husband was supporting her discreetly with one hand. The car started without a sound.

49

Maigret did not know that the Gymnase was having a first night, and he almost failed to get in. Municipal Guards were lined up on the pavement, and an awning stretched from the entrance to the kerb, where a small crowd had gathered, in spite of the rain, to watch the invited audience emerge from their cars.

The Superintendent had to ask to see the manager, and was kept hanging about in passages, looking conspicuous, the only man in a lounge suit.

'It's not that I object!' exclaimed the frenzied manager, waving his hands. 'But you are the twentieth person that's asked me for "a seat in a corner"! There isn't a seat left! And you're not even wearing a dinner-jacket!'

He was being summoned from all sides.

'You see! Put yourself in my shoes!'

In the end Maigret stood with his back to a door, among the usherettes and programme-sellers.

The Mortimer-Levingstons had a box. There were six people in it, including a princess and a cabinet minister. People went in and out. Hands were kissed and smiles exchanged.

The curtain rose to reveal a sunny garden. There were cries of 'Hush!' Whispers. Stumbling feet. Then the first actor's voice was heard, still hesitant but growing firmer, building up atmosphere.

But late-comers were still pushing in, and the cries of 'Hush!' began again. Somewhere, a woman tittered.

Mortimer-Levingston looked more aristocratic than ever. Evening dress suited him wonderfully, the white shirt-front setting off his sallow complexion.

Had he seen Maigret, or had he not? An usherette brought the Superintendent a stool, which he was obliged to share with a stout lady in black silk, the mother of one of the actresses.

First interval. Second interval. Comings and goings between the boxes. Spurious exhilaration. Greetings exchanged between the stalls and the dress circle.

The corridors, the foyer, and even the stairs were buzzing

like a hive of bees. Names were whispered, the names of maharajahs, financiers, statesmen, artists.

Mortimer-Levingston left his seat three times, appearing first in a stage box and then in the stalls, chatting with a former Prime Minister, whose booming laugh could be heard twenty rows away.

End of the third act. Flowers on the stage. An ovation for one skinny actress. The banging of tipped-up seats, the clatter of feet surging across the parquet.

When Maigret looked round at the Americans' box, Mortimer-Levingston had vanished.

Fourth and last act. This was the time for anyone who had any pretext for doing so to make for the wings and the actors' and actresses' dressing-rooms. Other people were besieging the cloakrooms or worrying about cars and taxis.

Maigret wasted a good ten minutes hunting round the theatre. Then he had to go outside, hatless and coatless, to question the police, the commissionaire, and the Municipal Guards.

At last he was told that Mortimer's olive-green limousine had just left. Someone showed him where it had been parked, outside a dive frequented by programme-sellers.

The car had driven off towards the Porte Saint-Martin. The American had not collected his coat and hat.

There were groups of spectators outside, enjoying the fresh air in any spot where they could find shelter from the rain.

The Superintendent smoked his pipe, with his hands in his pockets and a stubborn, withdrawn, angry face. The bell began to ring. People streamed back into the theatre. Even the Municipal Guards disappeared, to watch the last act.

The Boulevards looked dishevelled, as they do at eleven o'clock at night. The streaks of rain falling past the street lamps were thinning. A cinema was spewing out its audience, while the staff turned out the lights and carried the notices inside before closing for the night.

People were gathered under a street lamp, waiting for a bus. When it came there were squabbles, because the queue-ticket dispenser had run out. A policeman intervened, and long after the bus had gone was still in heated argument with a fat indignant man.

At last a limousine glided alongside the kerb. Almost before it stopped, Mortimer-Levingston, bare-headed, still in his evening clothes, opened the door, bounded up the steps of the theatre, and disappeared into the warmly lighted corridor.

Maigret looked at the chauffeur, one-hundred-per-cent American, hard-featured, with a jutting jaw, motionless in his seat as though his uniform held him rigid.

The commissionaire opened one of the quilted doors just a crack. Mortimer-Levingston was standing up at the back of his box. An actor was speaking disjointed, sardonic phrases. The curtain fell. Flowers. A burst of applause.

A rush for the doors. Cries of 'Hush!' The actor announced the author's name, and then fetched him from the stage box to take a call.

Mortimer-Levingston was kissing some hands, shaking others, giving a hundred-franc tip to the woman who brought his coat and hat.

His wife was pale, with mauve circles under her eyes. After they got into the car there was a moment of indecision.

The couple were arguing. Mrs Mortimer-Levingston was protesting irritably. Her husband lit a cigarette and closed his lighter with an angry snap.

Finally he said something into the speaking-trumpet, and the car drove off, followed by Maigret's taxi.

It was half past twelve. Rue La Fayette. The whitish pillars of the Trinité church, surrounded by scaffolding. Rue de Clichy.

The limousine stopped in the rue Fontaine outside Pickwick's Bar. Commissionaire in blue and gold. Cloakroom. Red curtain held back; the sound of a tango.

Maigret followed and sat down near the door, at a table

which must always have been empty, for it stood right in the draught.

The Mortimer-Levingstons had sat down close to the jazz band. He was looking at the menu, giving his order. A professional dancer stopped in front of Mrs Mortimer-Levingston, with a low bow.

She rose and danced. Levingston's eyes followed her with a curious persistence. She exchanged a few words with her partner, but did not once glance towards the corner where Maigret was sitting.

Here, among the evening dresses and dinner-jackets, there were a few foreigners in informal dress.

The Superintendent waved away a dance hostess who made as if to sit down at his table. The compulsory bottle of champagne was placed before him.

Paper festoons dangled everywhere. Balls of cotton wool were flying through the air. One hit Maigret on the nose, and he scowled at the old lady who had thrown it at him.

Mrs Mortimer-Levingston had returned to her seat. Her partner roamed round the floor and then made for the exit, lighting a cigarette.

Suddenly he lifted a corner of the red velvet curtain, and disappeared. About three minutes elapsed before it occurred to Maigret to put his head outside.

The dancer was not there.

The rest of the evening was long and dreary. The Mortimer-Levingstons ate a copious supper – caviar, *truffes au champagne, homard à l'américaine*, cheese.

Mrs Mortimer-Levingston did not dance again.

Maigret hated champagne, but he sipped it because he was thirsty. There were some salted almonds on his table; unfortunately he ate them, and they parched his tongue.

He looked at his watch: two o'clock.

The nightclub was emptying now. A girl dancer did her number, which was received with complete indifference. A drunken foreigner with three women at his table was making more noise than all the rest of the customers put together.

The dance partner, who had returned after a quarter of an

hour, had partnered several other ladies. But now it was ove
The place had an air of weariness.

Mrs Mortimer-Levingston was grey-faced, with droopir
eyelids.

Her husband beckoned to the attendant, who brought he
fur wrap and his overcoat and opera hat.

Maigret had the impression that the dancer, standing besi
the saxophonist, was watching him anxiously, while makir
conversation.

He summoned the *maître d'hôtel*, who kept him waiting,
that several moments were lost.

When the Superintendent finally got outside, the Amer
cans' car was turning the corner of the rue Notre-Dame-d
Lorette. Half a dozen empty taxis were waiting at the kerb.

He went towards one of them.

A shot rang out, and Maigret put his hand to his che
looked round, saw nothing, but heard footsteps hurryir
away down the rue Pigalle.

He went on for several yards, as though propelled by b
own momentum. The doorman ran up to support hir
People were coming out of Pickwick's to see what had ha
pened. Among them, Maigret noticed the tense face of th
male dancer.

# CHAPTER 7

# Maigret Gives Up the Game

ᵀAXI drivers who work the night shift in Montmartre understand at the slightest hint – often, indeed with no explanation at
all.

When the shot was fired, one of those waiting outside
Pickwick's Bar had been about to open the door of his cab for
Maigret. He did not know the Superintendent, but may have
guessed from his bearing that he was a police officer.

People were running from a small café across the street.
In a few seconds there would be quite a crowd surrounding
the wounded man. At this point the driver sprang to the aid
of the doorman, who was holding Maigret up but did not
know what to do with him. And in less than half a minute the
taxi was driving away, with Maigret inside.

The taxi drove straight on for about ten minutes, and then
stopped in an empty street. The driver got out, opened the
door, and saw his passenger sitting in an almost natural position, with one hand inside his jacket.

'I see it's nothing serious; I thought not. Where shall I take
you?'

Maigret looked rather upset, nevertheless – precisely
because the wound was only superficial. The bullet had torn
the flesh on his chest, grazed past a rib, and come out again
near the shoulder-blade.

'Police Headquarters.'

The driver grunted something inaudible. On the way, the
Superintendent changed his mind.

'Take me to the Majestic – the tradesmen's entrance, in the
Rue de Ponthieu.'

He had rolled his handkerchief into a ball and pressed it
against the wound, and now he found the bleeding had
stopped.

As they drove on towards the heart of Paris, his face began to show less pain and more anxiety.

The driver offered to help him out of the taxi, but he waved the man away and crossed the pavement with a firm step. He found the night porter dozing behind the window of his cubby-hole in the narrow passage.

'Has anything happened?'

'What do you mean?'

It was cold. Maigret went back to pay the taxi driver, who grumbled again at receiving only a hundred francs after his remarkable feat.

Even now Maigret made an impressive figure. The hand clutching the handkerchief was still pressed against his chest under his coat. He held one shoulder higher than the other and he was careful to husband his strength. He felt a bit light headed. Sometimes he felt that he was wavering, and had to make an effort to pull himself together, to recover his usual exactness of perception and movement.

He went up an iron staircase, opened a door, found himself in a passage, lost his way in a labyrinth of corridors, and ended up on another staircase, identical with the first but bearing a different number.

He had lost his way in the back corridors of the hotel. Fortunately he ran into a white-capped assistant cook, who watched his approach with great alarm.

'Show me the way to the first floor – the room next to M. Mortimer-Levingston's suite.'

But the young cook did not know the guests by name and he was upset at the sight of the five streaks of blood Maigret had left on his face when he had rubbed his hand over it.

This giant roaming about in the narrow service corridors with a black overcoat slung from his shoulders, the empty sleeves dangling, and one hand resting motionless on his chest, making a bulge under his jacket and waistcoat, quite terrified the young man.

'Police!' said Maigret impatiently.

He could feel dizziness coming over him. His wound was burning, as though long needles were stabbing through it.

In the end the cook set off, without a backward glance. A little later, Maigret felt a carpet under his feet. He realized that he was now out of the servants' quarters and in the hotel proper. He looked at the numbers of the rooms. He was on the odd-number side.

At last he met a scared chambermaid.

'Where is Mr Mortimer-Levingston's room?'

'On the floor below. . . . But . . . you . . .'

He went down one flight. Meanwhile a rumour was circulating among the staff that a strange, wounded, ghostly man was wandering about the hotel.

He leant against the wall for a moment and left a blood-stain on it, while three small drops, very dark red, fell on the carpet.

Eventually he found the Mortimer-Levingstons' suite, and next to it the door of the room Torrence was using. He went up to it, walking slightly askew, and pushed it open.

'Torrence!'

The lights were on. The table was still cluttered with plates of food and bottles.

Maigret's thick brows came together. He could not see his colleague. But there was a kind of hospital smell about the place.

He advanced a few paces, still feeling confused. And halted abruptly beside a sofa.

A foot in a black shoe was sticking out from under it.

He had to make three attempts. As soon as he took his hand away from his wound it began to bleed alarmingly.

Finally he seized the napkin which lay on the table, and pushed it inside his waistcoat, which he then buckled very tightly. The smell that hung about the room made him feel sick.

With fumbling hands he lifted a corner of the sofa and swivelled it on two legs.

As he had expected, it was Torrence that lay there, curled

up, with one arm twisted, as though they had broken his bones in order to cram him into a narrow space.

There was a bandage covering the lower part of his face but it was not tied. Maigret knelt down.

All his movements were steady, in fact very slow, no doubt because of his own condition. His hand seemed reluctant to feel the other man's chest. And when it reached the heart, the Superintendent froze and remained motionless, kneeling on the carpet, his eyes fixed on his companion.

Torrence was dead. Maigret's lips twitched imperceptibly. His fists clenched; his eyes clouded, and he uttered a terrible oath in the silent closed room.

It could have been ridiculous. But in fact it was terrible. Tragic. Terrifying.

Maigret's face had hardened. He was not weeping. He was probably incapable of that. But his features expressed such fury and grief, and such amazement, that he looked almost stupefied.

Torrence was 30 years old. For the last five years he had virtually been working solely with the Superintendent.

His mouth was open, as though in a desperate effort to get a breath of air.

On the floor above, just over the dead man's body, a hotel guest pulled off his shoes. Maigret glared round, looking for an enemy. He was breathing heavily.

Several minutes went by, and when Maigret rose to his feet it was because he could feel that something sinister was creeping through his own body.

He made his way to the window, opened it, and saw the Avenue des Champs-Élysées lying empty below. He let the breeze cool his forehead for a moment, and then went back to pick up the bandage he had taken off Torrence's face.

It was a damask table napkin, embroidered with the monogram of the Majestic. It still smelt faintly of chloroform. Maigret stood there, his mind a blank except for a few inchoate thoughts, which kept colliding in the vacuum and setting up grievous echoes.

Once again he leant his shoulder against the wall, as he had one in the corridor; and the lines of his face suddenly sagged. He looked old, disheartened. At that moment, perhaps, he came near to bursting into tears. But he was too tall, too massive, cast in too tough a mould.

The sofa was pulled sideways, touching the untidy table, where some cigarette-ends lay on a plate among chicken bones.

The Superintendent put out his hand towards the telephone. But he did not pick it up. With an angry snap of his fingers, he went back to the body and stood staring at it.

With a bitter, ironical grimace he reflected on the regulations, the Public Prosecutor's Department, the formalities, the precautions to be taken.

What did all that matter? This was Torrence! Almost a part of himself!

Torrence, a member of the firm, who . . .

He undid the man's waistcoat – so feverish beneath his apparent calm that he pulled off two buttons. And then he noticed something, and turned pale.

On the shirt front, level with the centre of the heart, there was a little brown speck.

Not even as big as a dried pea. Just one drop of blood had escaped, and had dried into a clot the size of a pinhead.

Maigret stared, misty-eyed, his face contorted with an indignation for which he could find no words.

It was horrible; but it revealed the true master-criminal. No need to search further. He knew the method, having read about it a few months previously in a German criminological magazine.

First the chloroform-soaked napkin, rendering the victim helpless in twenty or thirty seconds. Then the long needle, which the murderer unhurriedly drives in between two ribs, seeking the heart, plucking out its life silently and with no mess.

Precisely the same crime had been committed at Hamburg six months ago.

A bullet may go wide of the mark, or merely wound. Maigret was a proof of that. It makes both noise and mess.

A needle driven into the heart of a man lying inert kills him scientifically, with no possibility of error.

The Superintendent remembered something. That evening when the manager sent a message that the Mortimer-Leving stons were leaving for the theatre, he had been sitting on the radiator, gnawing the leg of a chicken and feeling suddenly so comfortable that he had almost decided to keep watch in the hotel himself and send Torrence to the theatre.

The thought upset him. He looked at his subordinate with embarrassment, feeling thoroughly uncomfortable, unable to decide whether it was because of his wound, his emotion, or the whiffs of chloroform.

The idea of opening a proper, official investigation did not even occur to him.

It was Torrence that lay there! Torrence, with whom he had been through every campaign in the last few years. Torrence, who understood him at the least word or sign.

Torrence; with his mouth open as though still trying to swallow a little oxygen, still trying to keep alive. And Maigret, unable to weep, felt ill, uneasy, sick at heart, with a weight on his shoulders.

He returned to the telephone and spoke into it, so softly that the operator had to ask him to repeat his number twice over.

'*Préfecture*. . . . Yes. Hello? *Préfecture?* . . . Who is that? Who? Tarraud? . . . Listen, my boy. Get over to the Chief's place. . . . Yes, to his home. . . . And tell him – tell him to come to me at the Majestic. Right away. Room . . . I don't know the number, but they'll show him. What? No, nothing else. . . .

'Hello. . . . What did you say? . . . No, I'm all right.'

He rang off, for the other man was asking questions, thinking his voice sounded strange and his instructions even stranger.

For a moment he stood there, arms hanging at his side. He kept his eyes averted from the corner where Torrence lay. Catching sight of himself in a mirror, he noticed that the

·od had soaked through the napkin. Then, with great
ïculty, he took off his jacket.

hour later the Director of the Criminal Investigation
partment knocked at the door, to which he had been led by
ıember of the hotel staff; it opened a crack, and he saw
igret peering out.

You can go,' said the Superintendent to the hotel em-
yee, in an expressionless voice.

ˋnd not until the man was out of sight did he open the door
ler. Only then did the Director see that Maigret was naked
the waist. The door into the bathroom stood wide open.
ere were pools of reddish water on the floor.

Shut the door quickly,' ordered the Superintendent, re-
dless of the other man's rank.

Vlaigret had a long purple gash on the right side of his
st. His braces were hanging down over his thighs.

ˋle jerked his head towards Torrence's corner, laid a finger
his lips and said: 'Sssh!'

ˋ shudder ran down the Director's spine:

Dead?' he queried in sudden alarm.

Vlaigret's head sank forward.

Will you lend me a hand, Chief?' he murmured sadly.

But . . . you. . . . It's very serious. . . .'

Ssh! . . . The bullet came out again, that's the main
ıg. . . . Help me to wrap all this up in the towel.'

ˋle had put the dinner dishes on the floor and cut the table-
th in two.

Pietr the Lett's gang,' he explained. 'They didn't get me.
t they got my lad Torrence. . . .'

Have you cleaned the wound?'

Yes. First with soap and then with iodine.'

You really think? . . .'

It'll do for the moment. . . . It was a needle, Chief. They
ed him with a needle, after putting him to sleep. . . .'

ˋle was a different man. It was like seeing and hearing
ı through a gauze curtain that blurred all sights and
ınds.

61

'Pass me my shirt. . . .'

A toneless voice. Measured, unsteady movements. A bla[ck]
face.

'It was essential that you should come. Seeing that it w[as]
one of us. Besides, I didn't want any fuss. Let them come a[nd]
fetch him presently. Not a word in the papers. You trust m[e,]
don't you, Chief?'

Yet there was a slight quiver in his voice. It touched t[he]
other man, who took him by the hand.

'Now then, Maigret! What's come over you?'

'Nothing. . . . I'm perfectly calm, I assure you. I don't thi[nk]
I have ever felt calmer. But now it's between them and m[e.]
You understand?'

The Director helped him on with his waistcoat and jack[et.]
Maigret looked deformed because of the bandage, whi[ch]
thickened his waist and made his figure bulge in places [as]
though he had rolls of fat.

He glanced at his reflection in the mirror, and pulled [an]
ironical face. He was well aware of his sloppy appearance. Th[is]
was not the formidable, flawless block of granite with whi[ch]
he liked to confront his adversaries.

His pale, blood-streaked face looked puffy, with a sugge[s]-
tion of bags under the eyes.

'Thanks, Chief. . . . You think it can be arranged, abo[ut]
Torrence?'

'To avoid publicity? Yes. . . . I'll tell the Public Pros[e]-
cutor. . . . I'll see him myself.'

'Good! Now I'll get to work.'

He said this as he tried to tidy his dishevelled hair. Then [he]
walked across to Torrence's body, hesitated, and asked [his]
companion:

'I can close his eyes, can't I? . . . I think he'd rather it w[as]
me. . . .'

His fingers were trembling. He kept them on the de[ad]
man's eyelids for a long moment, like a caress. The Direct[or,]
feeling the strain, called imploringly:

'Maigret!'

The Superintendent stood up and threw a last glance rou[nd]

n. 'Good-bye, Chief. ... Don't let them tell my wife I've
en hurt. ...'

For a second he stood in the doorway, entirely filling it.
e Director nearly called him back, feeling anxious about
n.

During the war, some of his fellow-soldiers had said good-
e to him like that, with the same tranquillity, the same un-
ural gentleness, before going into action.

And those were the ones that never came back.

CHAPTER 8

# The Killer

THE international gangs that specialize in large-scale swindl
seldom go in for killing.

One can even take it as axiomatic that they do not k
people, at any rate not those they have decided to relieve o'
large sum of money. Their thefts are committed by mo
scientific methods, and most of their associates are gentlem
who never handle a weapon.

But they do kill occasionally, to settle their own accoun
One or two insoluble murders are committed somewhere
other every year. In most cases the victim cannot be identifie
and is buried under a name known to be false.

It means he is either a traitor to the gang, a man wl
becomes talkative when he is drunk and has lapsed from d
cretion now and then, or a subordinate whose ambition is
threat to his bosses.

In America, the land of the specialist, executions of t
kind are never carried out by a member of the gang. Expe
known as 'killers' are called in; like State executioners, th
have their own assistants and their scale of fees.

It has sometimes been the same in Europe. Among oth
there was the notorious Polish gang whose leaders all end
on the scaffold; their services were enlisted several times
criminals of higher standing who did not wish to soil th
hands with blood.

Maigret was aware of this when he went downstairs a
across to the reception desk of the Majestic.

'When a visitor telephones for food, who takes the ca
he inquired.

'A special head waiter in charge of room service.'

'At night as well?'

'No. After nine o'clock it is a member of the night staff.'

'Who is to be found? . . .'

'In the basement.'

'Tell someone to take me there.'

Again he went behind the scenes of the luxury bee-hive designed for a thousand guests. He found an employee sitting at a switchboard in a room next to the kitchens. A ledger lay open in front of him. This was the slack time.

'Did Sergeant Torrence ring for you between nine o'clock yesterday evening and two o'clock this morning?'

'Torrence?'

'The police officer in the blue room, next to No. 3,' the clerk explained in professional terms.

'No, he didn't.'

'And no one went up there?'

The reasoning was elementary. Torrence had been attacked in that room, and therefore by someone who had gone in there. To gag his victim, the murderer must have been standing behind him. And Torrence had had no suspicion.

Nobody but a hotel waiter satisfied those conditions; he might have been sent for by Torrence, or he might have come of his own accord, to clear the table.

Showing no excitement, Maigret put his question in a different way.

'Which member of the staff went off duty early?'

The switchboard operator looked astonished.

'How did you know? What a coincidence! . . . Pepito had a phone call to say his brother was ill. . . .'

'What time was that?'

'About ten o'clock.'

'Where was he then?'

'Upstairs.'

'Which telephone did he take the call on?'

They rang through to the main switchboard. The operator on duty said he had passed no call to Pepito.

Things were moving quickly! But Maigret remained impassive and glum.

'Where is his card? You must have a card. . . .'

'Not exactly a card. . . . At least, not for what we call the dining-room staff. They change so often.'

They had to go to the secretary's office, which was empty at that hour. But Maigret had the books brought out, and found what he was looking for:

*Pepito Moretto, Hôtel Beauséjour, 3 rue des Batignolles. Took up service on . . .*

'Get me the Hôtel Beauséjour on the telephone.'

Meanwhile, questioning another employee, he learnt that Pepito Moretto, recommended by an Italian head waiter, had come to the Majestic three days before the Mortimer-Leving stons. His work had been perfectly satisfactory. He had begun in the dining-room and afterwards been transferred, at his own request, to room service.

The Hôtel Beauséjour came on the line.

'Hello. . . . Will you get me Pepito Moretto? Hello. . . What's that? . . . With his luggage? . . . Three o'clock in the morning? . . . Thank you. . . . Hello! . . . One more thing. Were his letters delivered at your hotel? . . . None at all? . . Thank you. That is all.'

And Maigret rang off, still maintaining his unnatural calm.

'What time is it?' he asked.

'Ten past five.'

'Call me a taxi.'

He told the driver to take him to Pickwick's Bar.

'It closes at four o'clock, you know?'

'Never mind.'

The taxi stopped outside the nightclub. The shutters were closed, but there was light showing under the door. Maigret knew that in most night spots the staff, who may number forty or more, usually have supper before going home.

They sit down to eat in the room the clients have just left, while the paper streamers are being swept up and the char women are beginning their work.

However, Maigret did not ring the bell at Pickwick's. Turning his back on the place, he noticed a *café-tabac* at the corner of the rue Fontaine, of the kind where nightclub staff are apt to congregate during the evening, between two jazz numbers or after closing-time.

This *bistro* was still open. When Maigret went in, three men were leaning on the bar, drinking coffee laced with brandy and talking shop.

'Isn't Pepito here?'

'He left a long time ago,' replied the *patron*.

The Superintendent noticed that one of the customers, who had perhaps recognized him, was signalling to the proprietor to keep quiet.

'I had an appointment with him for two o'clock,' he resumed.

'He was here then. . . .'

'I know. I sent him a message by one of the dancers across the road.'

'José?'

'That's it. He must have told Pepito I couldn't get away.'

'José did come, that's true. . . . I think they were talking together. . . .'

The customer who had made signs to the *patron* was now drumming with his fingers on the bar. He was pale with anger, for the few words that had slipped out were enough to explain what had happened.

At ten o'clock that night, or shortly before, Pepito had murdered Torrence at the Majestic.

He must have had very precise instructions, for he had immediately left his work, on the pretext that his brother had telephoned, and gone to the café at the corner of the rue Fontaine, where he had waited.

At a certain moment the dancer just referred to as José had crossed the street and given him a message, which was childishly obvious – he was to shoot Maigret the moment he came out of Pickwick's.

In other words, two crimes within a few hours. And the only two men who were dangerous to Pietr the Lett would be disposed of!

Pepito had fired his shot and run away, having played his

67

part. He had not been seen, so he could go and fetch his belongings from the Hôtel Beauséjour.

Maigret paid for his drink and left; glancing back he saw the three customers bombarding the *patron* with reproaches.

He knocked on the door of Pickwick's Bar, and it was opened by a charwoman.

As he had expected, the staff were at supper, seated round the tables, which had been lined up in a row. There were remains of chicken, partridge, dessert, whatever the clients had not finished off. Thirty heads turned towards the Superintendent.

'Is it long since José left?'

'Oh yes – directly after . . .'

But the head waiter recognized Maigret, whom he had waited upon himself, and he nudged the speaker with his elbow.

Maigret did not beat about the bush.

'Give me his address! The right one, or you'll be sorry.'

'I don't know. . . . Only the proprietor. . . .'

'Where is he?'

'Gone to his country place at La Varenne.'

'Give me the register.'

'But . . .'

'Quiet!'

They pretended to hunt through the drawers in a small office behind the orchestra platform. Maigret pushed them aside and at once found the ledger, where he read:

*José Latourie, 71 rue Lepic.*

He went out as he had come in, with a heavy step, while the waiters, still alarmed, resumed their meal.

He was only a few yards from the rue Lepic. But No. 71 is fairly high up the steep hill. He had to stop twice, out of breath. At last he came to the door of a hotel, similar to the Beauséjour but more squalid, and rang the bell. The door opened automatically. He knocked on a small round window in the corridor, and a sleepy night porter eventually emerged.

'José Latourie?'

The man looked at the row of keys hanging at the head of his bed.

'Not in yet. His key is here. . . .'

'Give it to me. Police.'

'But . . .'

'Quick!'

The fact was that no one opposed him that night. Yet he was not as stern and unbending as usual. But perhaps they sensed vaguely that this was worse.

'Which floor?'

'Fourth.'

The room was long, narrow and stuffy. The bed was unmade. José, like most of his kind, must have stayed in bed till four o'clock in the afternoon, after which hour hotel-keepers refuse to have rooms done.

An old pyjama jacket, threadbare at the neck and elbows, was lying on the sheet. On the floor was a pair of dancing pumps, trodden down at the back and with holes in the soles, now used as bedroom slippers.

A travelling bag in imitation leather contained only some old newspapers and a pair of patched black trousers.

Above the wash-basin lay a cake of soap, a pot of ointment, a few aspirins, and a tube of veronal.

On the ground was a screw of paper which Maigret picked up and carefully unfolded. One sniff was enough to inform him that it had contained heroin.

Fifteen minutes later, after hunting everywhere, he noticed a hole in the rep cover of the only arm-chair, pushed his finger into it, and pulled out, one by one, eleven packets of the same drug, each containing one gramme.

He put them in his wallet and went downstairs. In the Place Blanche he approached a policeman, to whom he gave certain instructions. The constable went up the rue Lepic and stationed himself near No. 71.

Maigret remembered the black-haired young man, a sickly shifty-eyed gigolo who had bumped into his table in his agitation, after going out to speak to Moretto.

He had been afraid to go home when the thing was over, preferring to sacrifice his three miserable suits and the eleven small packets – though at the retail price these would be worth at least a thousand francs.

He would be caught one day, for his nerve was poor and he must be haunted by fear.

Pepito was infinitely more self-possessed. He might be waiting on some station platform to catch the first train. He might have gone to ground in the suburbs, or simply have moved to a hotel in another district.

Maigret hailed a taxi and almost gave the address of the Majestic. But he calculated that they would not yet have finished there. In other words, Torrence would still be in that room.

'Quai des Orfèvres,' he said.

Walking past Jean, he realized that the man already knew what had happened, and he turned his head aside almost guiltily.

He paid no attention to his stove. He did not take off his jacket or his shirt collar.

For two hours he sat motionless, with his elbows on the desk, and it was daylight by the time it occurred to him to look at a paper which must have been put there during the night.

'To Superintendent Maigret. Urgent.

'A man in evening dress came to the Hôtel du Roi de Sicile about eleven-thirty and remained for ten minutes. He left again in a private car. The Russian has not been out.'

Maigret's expression did not change. And now, news came pouring in. First there was a telephone call from the police station in the Courcelles district.

'A certain José Latourie, a professional dancing-partner, has been found dead outside the gate of the Parc Monceau. He had three knife wounds. His wallet had not been stolen. The time and circumstances of the crime are unknown.'

Not to Maigret. He could imagine them at once. Pepito Moretto coming up behind the young man as he left Pickwick's, thinking he was too upset and liable to give the show away, killing him without even bothering to take his wallet and identity papers – perhaps out of bravado.

'You think you can trace us through him? Well, here he is!' Pepito seemed to be saying.

Half past eight. The voice of the manager of the Majestic came over the telephone.

'Hello? . . . Superintendent Maigret? . . . It's incredible, preposterous! . . . A few minutes ago there was a ring from No. 17. No. 17! . . . You remember? The room that . . .'

'That Oswald Oppenheim was in. Yes. Well?'

'I sent a waiter along. . . . Oppenheim was lying in bed as though nothing had happened, and he asked for his breakfast. . . .'

# CHAPTER 9

## *Oswald Oppenheim's Return*

MAIGRET had been sitting still for two hours. When he tried to stand up he could scarcely move his arms, and he had to ring for Jean to help him on with his coat.

'Get a taxi for me.'

A few minutes later he walked into Dr Lecourbe's house in the rue Monsieur-le-Prince. There were six people in the waiting-room, but he was taken round, through the flat, and as soon as the consulting room was free he went in.

It was an hour before he came out again. He was carrying himself more stiffly than before, and the rings round his eyes had darkened so much that his whole expression had altered as though he had made up his face.

'Rue du Roi-de-Sicile. I'll tell you when to stop.'

From a distance he saw his two inspectors patrolling outside the hotel. He got out of the taxi and joined them.

'He's not come out?'

'No. One or the other of us has been here all the time.'

'Who has left the hotel?'

'A little bent-up old man, and then two young chaps, and then a woman of about thirty. . . .'

Maigret asked, with a shrug and a sigh:

'Had the old man got a beard?'

'Yes. . . .'

He left them without a word, and went up the narrow staircase and past the lodge. A moment later he was rattling the door of Room 32. A woman's voice replied in an unknown language. The door gave way, and he saw Anna Gorski getting out of bed, half naked.

'Where's your boy-friend?' he demanded.

He spoke curtly, like a man in a hurry, not bothering to look round the place.

'Get out! . . . You have no right! . . .' shouted the woman.

But he, impassive, bent to pick up the familiar trench-coat from the floor. He seemed to be looking for something else. He saw Fédor Yurovich's greyish trousers at the foot of the bed.

There were no man's shoes in the room, however.

Anna, who was struggling into her dressing-gown, stared at him ferociously.

'You think because we're foreigners . . .'

He did not wait for her burst of rage. He went out calmly, closing the door, which she reopened before he had gone down one flight of stairs. She stood on the landing, breathing heavily, without a word. She leant over the banisters to watch him, and suddenly, unable to restrain her irresistible urge to do something, anything, she spat.

The spittle fell with a soft splash, missing him by a couple of inches.


'Well? . . .' asked Inspector Dufour.

'Watch the woman. *She* won't be able to disguise herself as an old man. . . .'

'You mean to say that? . . .'

Oh no – he didn't mean to say anything! He was in no mood for argument. He got back into his taxi.

'The Majestic.'

Uneasy and humiliated, the inspector watched him go.

'Do what you can!' called Maigret.

He didn't want to hurt the man's feelings, either. It wasn't his fault that he had been tricked. Hadn't Maigret himself allowed Torrence to be killed?


The manager was waiting for him at the entrance, which indicated an entirely new attitude.

'Well. . . . You understand. . . . I don't know what to do next. . . . They came and fetched your . . . your friend. . . . They assured me that nothing would appear in the papers. . . . But the *other man* is here. *Here!*'

'No one saw him come in?'

73

'No one. That's just what ... Listen. I told you on the telephone, he rang his bell. ... When the waiter went in, he ordered coffee. He was in bed. ...'

'And Mortimer-Levingston?'

'You think there is a connexion? Impossible! He's a celebrity. ... Cabinet ministers and bankers have called on him at this very hotel! ...'

'What is Oppenheim doing now?'

'He has just had a bath. I think he is getting dressed.'

'And Mortimer-Levingston?'

'The Mortimer-Levingstons haven't rung yet. They are still asleep.'

'Give me a description of Pepito Moretto.'

'Oh yes. ... I was told ... Personally, I never saw him. Not to notice him, I mean. We have such a large staff! But I have made inquiries. A small, swarthy, black-haired, stocky man, who never said a word from one day to the next. ...'

Maigret wrote this down on a sheet of paper and put it into an envelope which he addressed to his chief. With the fingerprints that must certainly have been found in the rooms where Torrence was killed, that ought to be enough.

'Have this taken to the Préfecture.'

'Yes, Superintendent.'

The manager had become positively suave, for he felt that the affair might take on disastrous proportions.

'What are you going to do?'

But the Superintendent was already walking away, with an awkward chunky gait. He stopped in the middle of the hall, looking like a visitor to some historic church who is trying to guess, without the verger's help, what interesting features it possesses.

A ray of sunshine appeared, and the hall of the Majestic glittered like gold.

At nine o'clock in the morning it was practically deserted. A few people were having breakfast at widely scattered tables, reading their newspapers.

After a time Maigret sank into a cane chair beside the little fountain, which for some reason was not working that day. The goldfish in the ceramic pool remained obstinately motionless, merely opening and shutting their mouths vacantly.

This reminded the Superintendent of Torrence's open mouth. The recollection must have distressed him considerably, because he shifted about for a long time before finding a position that suited him.

A few servants were coming and going. Maigret followed them with his eyes, aware that a shot might be fired at any moment.

The issue had become as crucial as that.

The fact that Maigret had identified Oppenheim as Pietr the Lett was of no great consequence, and he was not in much danger from that.

Pietr was at no pains to hide himself, he was defying the police, convinced that they could bring no charge against him.

To prove him right, there was that series of telegrams following him step by step from Cracow to Bremen, Bremen to Amsterdam, Amsterdam to Brussels, and Brussels to Paris.

But then there had been the dead man on the *North Star*. And above all there had been Maigret's discovery that there was an unexpected connexion between Pietr the Lett and Mortimer-Levingston.

That discovery had brought matters to a head.

Pietr was a self-confessed bandit, who simply said to the international police:

'Catch me at it if you can!'

Whereas Mortimer-Levingston was universally regarded as a pillar of respectability.

There were two people who might have guessed the relationship between Pietr and Mortimer-Levingston.

And that very evening, Torrence had been killed and Maigret shot at in the rue Fontaine.

A third person, hapless and probably knowing little or nothing, but a possible starting-point for a new investigation, had also been liquidated – José Latourie, the gigolo.

Now Mortimer-Levingston and the Lett, their confidence

presumably restored by the triple murder, had gone back to their places. There they were, upstairs in their luxurious suites, giving orders by telephone to the staff of a great hotel, taking baths, having breakfast, getting dressed.

Maigret was waiting for them all by himself, seated uncomfortably in a cane arm-chair, one side of his chest stiff and throbbing, his right arm almost paralysed by a dull ache.

He had the power to arrest them. But he knew it would be no use. It might conceivably be possible to collect evidence against Pietr the Lett, alias Fédor Yurovich, alias Oswald Oppenheim – who had doubtless been known by plenty of other names as well, perhaps including that of Olaf Swaan.

But against Mortimer-Levingston, the American multi-millionaire? Within an hour of his arrest there would be a protest from the United States Ambassador. The French banks and the many companies of which he was a director would make a stir in political circles.

What proof? What clue? The fact that he had walked off for a few hours in the wake of Pietr the Lett?

That he had gone to Pickwick's for supper, and his wife had danced with José Latourie?

That a police inspector had seen him go into a squalid hotel called the Roi de Sicile?

All that would be torn to shreds! Apologies would have to be offered, and even steps taken, such as dismissing Maigret – ostensibly, at any rate – as a sop to the United States.

Torrence was dead!

He must have passed through this hall, on a stretcher, as dawn began to break. Unless the manager, anxious not to confront any early-rising client with a painful sight, had persuaded the stretcher-bearers to go out through the servants' quarters.

Probably he had. The narrow passages, the winding stairs, where the stretcher must have banged into the hand-rail.

The telephone rang, behind the mahogany counter.

People bustling to and fro. Flurried orders.

The manager came over.

'Mrs Mortimer-Levingston is leaving. . . . They have just

76

rung down for her trunk to be fetched. . . . The car has arrived.'

Maigret smiled frostily.

'What train?' he asked.

'She is catching the Berlin plane from Le Bourget.'

Before he had finished speaking she appeared, wearing a greyish travelling coat and carrying a crocodile handbag. She was walking quickly. But on reaching the revolving door she could not resist a backward glance.

To make certain that she saw him, Maigret rose, with an effort. He was positive that she bit her lip and went out still more hurriedly, gesticulating as she gave her orders to the chauffeur.

The manager was called away. The Superintendent was left alone, standing beside the fountain, which suddenly began to work. There must be a fixed time for turning the water on.

It was ten o'clock.

He smiled again, to himself, and sat down heavily but cautiously, for his wound was becoming more and more painful, and hurt him at the slightest movement.

'They're getting rid of the weaklings. . . .'

For that was it, right enough! After José Latourie, who had been regarded as unstable and dismissed from the scene with three knife-stabs in the chest, they were getting rid of Mrs Mortimer-Levingston, who might also be intimidated. She was being sent to Berlin. That was privileged treatment!

The tough nuts remained: Pietr the Lett, who was taking an interminable time to get dressed; Mortimer-Levingston, who had doubtless lost nothing of his aristocratic bearing; and Pepito Moretto, the gang's 'killer'.

All of them, linked by invisible threads, were getting ready.

The enemy was there, in their midst, in the middle of the hall, where signs of life were now beginning to appear. He was sitting motionless in a wicker arm-chair, with his legs stretched out, while the fountain tinkled close by and its fine spray blew into his face like dust.

One of the lifts came down and stopped.

Pietr the Lett was the first to emerge, wearing a superb cinnamon-coloured suit and with a Henry Clay between his lips.

He was at home here. He was paying for it. Casual, self-assured, he strolled round the hall, pausing here and there in front of the showcases which the big shops maintain in luxury hotels. He asked one of the page-boys for a light, he inspected a board on which the latest foreign exchange rates were posted up; he came to a halt within three yards of Maigret, beside the fountain, staring fixedly at the artificial-looking goldfish. Finally he flicked the ash from his cigar into the pool, and walked off towards the reading-room.

# A Restless Way

PIETR THE LETT glanced through several newspapers, paying particular attention to the *Revaler Bote*, an Estonian periodical of which the Majestic had only one old copy, presumably left by some departing guest.

Shortly before eleven o'clock he lit another cigar, walked across the hall, and sent a page-boy to fetch his hat.

Thanks to the sunshine flooding on to one side of the Champs-Élysées, it was fairly warm outside.

Pietr went out wearing a grey felt hat and no overcoat, and strolled slowly up to the Étoile, like a man just taking a breath of air.

Maigret followed at a short distance, making no attempt to conceal himself. He did not find the walk enjoyable, for his movements were hampered by the dressing on his chest.

At the corner of the rue de Berry he heard a faint whistle a few steps away, but paid no attention. The whistle was repeated. At this he looked round, and saw Inspector Dufour, making mysterious signs to indicate that he had something to tell his chief.

The Inspector was standing in the rue de Berry, pretending to be engrossed in the contemplation of a chemist's window, so that his gestures seemed to be addressed to the wax head of a woman, one cheek of which was carefully covered with eczema.

'Come here! Come along! Quick. . . .' said Maigret.

Dufour was hurt and offended. For the last hour he had been prowling in the vicinity of the Majestic, employing the most cunning ruses, and now the Superintendent was ordering him to show himself in broad daylight!

'What's going on?'

'It's that Gorskin woman. . . .'

'Gone out?'

'She's here. . . . And now you've made me come forward, she can see us both at this moment. . . .'

Maigret looked round him.

'Where is she?'

'The Select. . . . She's sitting inside. . . . Look, though: the curtain's moving. . . .'

'Keep watching.'

'Without hiding myself?'

'Go and drink an *apéritif* at the table next to hers, if you like.'

As matters now stood in this contest, it would be pointless to play hide-and-seek. Maigret walked on. After two hundred yards he again saw Pietr the Lett, who had not tried to exploit the conversation by dodging away.

Why should he? The game was being played on new ground. The opponents could see one another. The cards were practically on the table.

Pietr went twice up and down from the Étoile to the Rond-Point des Champs-Élysées, and in the end Maigret knew every smallest detail of his appearance, had summed up his physical characteristics in full.

Physically Pietr was elegant, fine-drawn, in fact with more distinction than Mortimer-Levingston, for instance; but his was a Nordic type of distinction.

The Superintendent had studied several men of that kind, all intellectuals. And his Latin mind had been thoroughly perplexed by those he had known in the Latin quarter, during a period of medical studies which he had not completed.

He remembered one of them, a thin, blond Pole; at the age of 22 he had already shown signs of incipient baldness; back in his own country his mother was a charwoman; and for seven solid years he had attended lectures at the Sorbonne with no socks on his feet, and with literally nothing to eat but a piece of bread and one egg, day after day.

As he could not afford to buy the set books, he had been forced to study in the public libraries.

He knew nothing about Paris, about women, or about the French character. But almost before his studies were completed, he was offered an important professorship at Warsaw University. Five years later, Maigret saw him again in Paris, as aloof, short-spoken, and cold as ever; he was a member of a delegation of foreign scientists, and he dined with the President.

The Superintendent had known others of his kind. Not all of them were of equal quality. But nearly all were astonishing, because of the number and variety of things they wanted to learn and did learn.

Study for the sake of study! Like that Belgian university professor who knew all the Far Eastern dialects (some forty of them), but had never set foot in Asia and was not in the least interested in the nations whose languages he analysed in his dilettante way.

The grey-green eyes of Pietr the Lett expressed that kind of determination. And yet, no sooner had one decided to classify him with the race of intellectuals than one noticed other points which reopened the whole question.

It was as though the shadow of Fédor Yurovich, the Russian vagabond in the trench-coat, were cast over the clear-cut figure at the Majestic.

That they were one and the same man was already a moral certainty and fast becoming a material one.

On the evening he arrived in Paris, Pietr had vanished. Next morning Maigret had found him at Fécamp, in the guise of Fédor Yurovich.

He had gone to the Hôtel du Roi de Sicile. A few hours later, Mortimer-Levingston had visited the hotel. Several people had come out after that, including an old, bearded man. And in the morning, Pietr the Lett had been back again at the Majestic.

The astounding thing was that apart from a rather striking physical resemblance the two personalities had absolutely nothing in common.

Fédor Yurovich was unmistakably a vagabond Slav, a melancholy, rock-bottom down-and-out. Not one false note.

Not one slip, for instance, while he was leaning on the bar i
that low dive at Fécamp.

On the other hand there was not a flaw in the personali
of Pietr the Lett – a well-bred intellectual from head to foot, i
his manner of asking a page-boy for a light, in the angle
which he wore his grey felt hat – which was of the be
English make – in his nonchalant manner of savouring th
sunlit air of the Champs-Élysées or looking at a shop windo

And this perfection was not just superficial. Maigret kne
what it was to play a part: the police do not disguise them
selves and make up their faces as often as people think, but
has to be done at times.

But Maigret in disguise was still Maigret in certain way
certain facial expressions or mannerisms.

Maigret as a big cattle-dealer, for instance (he had done tha
and brought it off) would be *acting* the cattle-dealer. But M
would not *be* one. He would never get into the skin of the par

Whereas Pietr–Fédor was Pietr or Fédor through an
through.

In short, the Superintendent's impression was that the ma
was both characters at one and the same time, not only
get-up but in essence.

He had been alternating between these two utterly differe
lives, no doubt for a long time, perhaps from the very first.

These were only disconnected ideas, flowing in on Maigr
while he walked slowly along, relishing the mild atmospher

But all of a sudden the Lett's personality splintered.

The circumstances that led to this were significant. He ha
come to a halt opposite Fouquet's, and even begun to cro
the Champs-Élysées, with the obvious intention of taking a
*apéritif* at the bar of that fashionable establishment.

But he changed his mind, went on along the same side
the avenue, and suddenly, quickening his pace, darted into th
rue Washington.

In that street there is a *bistro* of the type to be found in th
heart of all the wealthiest districts, serving taxi-drivers an
domestic servants.

Pietr went in. The Superintendent followed close behind, just as he was ordering an absinthe substitute.

He was standing by the horseshoe-shaped bar, which a blue-aproned waiter wiped from time to time with a dirty cloth. To his left was a group of dusty bricklayers. To his right, a man in the uniform of the gas company.

Pietr looked thoroughly out of place, with his air of refinement and the quiet, flawless elegance of his clothes.

His little toothbrush moustache and his thin eyebrows looked too blond and glistening. He was staring at Maigret, not face to face, but in a mirror.

And the Superintendent noted that his lips were quivering, his nostrils imperceptibly narrowed.

Pietr must be watching his step. At first he drank slowly, but soon he gulped down what remained in his glass and jerked his finger in a way that meant:

'Fill it up!'

Maigret had ordered a vermouth. In this little bar he looked even taller and bulkier than usual. He never took his eyes off Pietr.

In a way, he was in two places at once. Two pictures were overlaid, as they had been a few minutes earlier. The squalid café at Fécamp formed a backcloth to the present scene. Pietr was a double figure. Maigret saw him simultaneously in his light-brown suit and in a shabby raincoat.

'I tell yer I ain't puttin' up with it no longer!' said one of the bricklayers, banging his glass on the counter.

Pietr was drinking his third opal-coloured *apéritif*; the smell of aniseed drifted into Maigret's nostrils.

The gas man had shifted his position in such a way that Maigret and Pietr were now side by side, their elbows touching.

Maigret was two heads taller than the other man. They were both facing a mirror, and staring at each other in its grey, limpid surface.

The Lett's eyes were the first of his features to become blurred. He snapped his thin white fingers, pointed to his glass, and passed a hand across his forehead.

And then, little by little, a kind of battle began in his face. At one moment it was the features of the Majestic's client that Maigret saw in the mirror; then it was the harassed face of Anna Gorskin's lover.

But this second face never came right to the surface. It was thrust back by a desperate muscular effort. Only the eyes were always Fédor's eyes.

The man's left hand was clinging to the edge of the counter. His body swayed to and fro.

Maigret tried an experiment. In his pocket was the picture of Madame Swaan that he had taken from the Fécamp photographer's album.

'What do I owe you?' he asked the waiter.

'Two francs twenty.'

He pretended to be hunting in his wallet, and dropped the photo, which fell into a puddle between the up-curved edges of the counter.

He ignored it, and held out a five-franc note. But he was staring hard into the mirror.

The waiter had picked up the photograph and, with profuse apologies, was wiping it on his apron.

Pietr the Lett stood there stony-eyed, clutching his glass. Not a muscle moved in his face.

Then, suddenly, there was a faint, unexpected sound, so sharp that the *patron*, busy at the cash desk, swung round on his heel.

Pietr's hand opened, and the fragments of his glass fell on the counter.

He had crushed it to pieces, slowly. Blood was trickling from a narrow cut on his forefinger.

He threw down a hundred-franc note in front of him and walked out, not glancing at Maigret.

Now he was making straight for the Majestic. No trace of intoxication. His appearance was the same as when he set out, his step as firm.

Stubbornly, Maigret followed at his heels. Coming in sight

the hotel, he saw a car drive away, and recognized it. It was
the car of the Judicial Identification Service, removing the
police cameras and the apparatus which had been used to
detect finger-prints.

This encounter took the wind out of his sails. For a second
he lost confidence, as though he were drifting, with nothing
to hold on to.

He went past the Select. Through the window, Inspector
Dufour made a signal which was supposed to be confidential,
but in fact drew all eyes unerringly to Anna Gorskin's table.

'Mortimer-Levingston?' queried the Superintendent, pausing at the reception desk of the hotel.

'He has just left by car for the American Embassy, where he
is lunching.'

Pietr the Lett went to his own table in the dining-room,
which was empty.

'Will you be lunching too?' the manager asked Maigret.

'Yes – put me at his table.'

The manager nearly choked.

'At his ... That's not possible! The room is completely
empty, and ...'

'I said at his table.'

Unwilling to admit defeat, the manager ran after Maigret.

'Listen! He's sure to make a scene. ... I can put you somewhere where you'll be able to see him just as well.'

'I said at his table.'

It was then, as he strolled about in the hall, that he noticed
he was tired. A subtle fatigue that was affecting his whole
body, in fact his whole being, flesh and spirit alike.

He dropped into the wicker arm-chair where he had sat
earlier in the morning. A couple consisting of a lady of very
ripe years and an over-elegant young man rose at once, and
the woman, fidgeting irritably with her lorgnette, said in a
voice loud enough to be overheard:

'These big hotels are becoming impossible. Just look at
that. ...'

'That' was Maigret, who couldn't even raise a smile.

# CHAPTER II

# The Woman with the Revolver

'HELLO? . . . Hm . . . It *is* you, isn't it?'

'Maigret speaking, yes,' sighed the Superintendent, wh[...]
had recognized the voice of Inspector Dufour.

'Shh . . . I'll be brief, Chief. . . . She went to the ladies. .[...]
Left handbag on table. . . . I went over . . . . Revolver in it.'

'Is she still there?'

'Yes, eating. . . .'

Dufour, in the telephone box, must be looking conspir[...]
torial, making cryptic gestures of alarm. Maigret rang [...]
without comment. He hadn't the heart to reply. These litt[...]
eccentricities, which usually amused him, now gave him [...]
kind of nausea.

The manager had resignedly ordered a place to be la[...]
opposite Pietr, who was already at the table and had asked t[...]
head waiter:

'Who is that place for?'

'I don't know, Monsieur. Those are my orders. . . .'

And he had not pursued the point. An English family [...]
five now came noisily into the dining-room and took some [...]
the chill out of the atmosphere.

Leaving his hat and heavy overcoat with an attendar[...]
Maigret walked across the room and paused before sittir[...]
down, even giving the ghost of a bow.

But Pietr did not appear to notice him. The four or fi[...]
*apéritifs* he had swallowed were forgotten. He was co[...]
punctilious, his movements were precise.

Not for a second did he show the least sign of nerves; h[...]
abstracted gaze looked more like that of an engineer with [...]
technical problem on his mind.

He drank little, but he had chosen one of the best bu[...]
gundies of the last twenty years.

He ate sparingly: omelet *aux fines herbes*, escalope, and *crème fraîche*.

Between courses he sat with his hands folded on the table, waiting with no sign of impatience, heedless of what went on around him.

The dining-room was filling up.

'Your moustache is coming unstuck,' said Maigret suddenly.

Pietr showed no sign of having heard; only, after a moment, he brushed his upper lip casually with two fingers. It was true, though hardly perceptible.

The Superintendent's calm was a byword at the Préfecture, but now even he had some difficulty in keeping his composure.

And during the remainder of the afternoon it was to be sorely tried.

Not that he had expected Pietr to make any compromising move before his very eyes.

But in the morning he had seemed to show the first signs of a breakdown. Might there not be some hope of driving him beyond his limit, by the perpetual presence of Maigret's bulk, looming like an immovable barrier between him and the light?

The Lett took coffee in the hall, sent upstairs for a light overcoat, strolled down the Champs-Élysées, and, a little after two o'clock, went into a neighbouring cinema.

He stayed there until six o'clock, without exchanging a word with anyone, writing anything, or making the slightest ambiguous move.

Leaning back in his seat, he attentively followed the plot of a trivial film. When, after this, he was walking to the Place de l'Opéra, where he took an *apéritif*, had he glanced round he would have noticed that Maigret was showing signs of wilting. He might even have sensed that the Superintendent was beginning to lose his self-confidence.

So much so, that during the hours spent in the dark, staring at the screen with its fleeting images, which he made no attempt to follow, Maigret had all the time been contemplating the possibility of making an immediate arrest.

But he knew so well what would happen if he did! There was no conclusive material evidence. And a whole barrage of influences would instantly be brought to bear on the examining magistrate, the Public Prosecutor, even the Foreign Minister and the Minister of Justice!

He was walking with his shoulders slightly bent, his wound was smarting, and his right arm growing stiffer and stiffer. And the doctor had told him very seriously:

'If the pain spreads, come here as quickly as you can. It means that the wound is becoming infected. . . .'

And if it did? As though he had time to think about that!

'Just look at that!' a woman at the Majestic had exclaimed before lunch.

Well, yes. 'That' was a police officer, trying to prevent a group of big criminals from continuing their exploits, and determined to avenge a colleague who had been murdered in that very hotel!

'That' was a man who did not get his clothes from a London tailor, who had no time to have his hands manicured every morning, and whose wife had been cooking wasted meals for him for the last three days, resigned to knowing nothing of his whereabouts.

'That' was a senior police Superintendent, with a salary of two thousand two hundred francs a month, who, once he had finished a case and the murderers were behind bars, had to sit down with a sheet of paper in front of him, make out a list of his expenses, attach all the receipts and vouchers, and then argue it out with the cashier!

Maigret had no car, no fortune, no staff of assistants. And if he did venture to use the services of one or two police officers, he had to explain, afterwards, why he had needed them.

Pietr the Lett, sitting three yards away, paid for his *apéritif* with a fifty-franc note and left the change. It was a mania with him, or a form of bluff. Then he went into a men's shop and, no doubt for the fun of it, spent half an hour selecting twelve ties and three dressing-gowns, laid his card on the counter, and left, escorted to the door by a faultlessly-attired salesman.

The wound must definitely be getting inflamed. Sometimes great stabs shot through Maigret's shoulder, and he had a sick feeling in his chest, as though his stomach were involved in the business.

Rue de la Paix. Place Vendôme. Faubourg Saint-Honoré. Pietr the Lett strolled on. . . .

At last the Majestic, where the page-boys rushed forward to spin the revolving door for him.

'Chief . . .'

'You again?'

Inspector Dufour stepped hesitantly out of the shadows, looking careworn.

'Listen. . . . She's disappeared. . . .'

'What on earth do you mean?'

'I did my best, I swear I did! She walked out of the Select. A moment later she went into No. 52, a dress shop. I waited an hour before asking the doorman. She had not been seen in the first-floor showroom. She'd simply walked through the building, which has another entrance in the rue de Berry. . . .'

'Very well.'

'What shall I do?'

'Take a rest.'

Dufour caught the Superintendent's eye and hastily averted his own.

'I do assure you . . .'

To his stupefaction, Maigret patted him on the shoulder.

'You're a good chap, Dufour. Just stop worrying old man.'

And he went into the Majestic, intercepted the manager's grimace and answered it with a smile.

'Pietr the Lett?'

'He has just gone up to his room.'

Maigret turned to one of the lifts.

'Second floor.'

He filled his pipe, and suddenly realized – smiling again, rather more sourly than before – that he had forgotten to smoke for several hours.

89

At the door of No. 17 he knocked without hesitation. A voice called to him to come in. He did so, closing the door behind him.

In spite of the central heating, there was a log fire in the sitting-room, by way of decoration. Pietr, leaning on the mantelpiece, was pushing a burning paper with his toe to hasten its destruction.

Maigret realized at a glance that the man was not so calm as before; but he had sufficient hold over himself to conceal his delight.

With one of his huge hands he grasped the back of a tiny gilded chair, which he carried to within a yard of the fire. There he set it down again on its spindle-legs and seated himself astride it.

Was it because he had his pipe between his teeth again? Or because his whole being had got its second wind after the recent hours of dejection, or rather indecision?

In any case, at that moment he looked larger than ever. He was double-strength Maigret, so to speak. A block hewn out of weathered oak, or solid rock.

He propped both elbows on the chair-back. He looked as though he would be capable, if driven beyond endurance, of seizing the other man's neck in one enormous hand and banging his head against the wall.

'Is Mortimer-Levingston back?' he rapped out.

Pietr, who was watching the paper burn, raised his head slowly. 'I don't know. . . .'

His fists were clenched, a point that did not escape Maigret. Nor did it escape him that a suitcase, which had not been in the suite before, was standing near the bedroom door.

It was a cheap travelling-case, worth about a hundred francs at most, and looked quite out of place in these surroundings.

'What's in that?'

No reply. But Pietr's face twitched nervously. After a moment he asked:

'Are you arresting me?'

And it almost seemed that beneath its anxiety his voice held a note of relief.

'Not yet.'

Maigret rose, went over to the suitcase, and pushed it with his toe to the fireplace, where he opened it.

Inside was a brand-new ready-made grey suit; someone had forgotten to unpick the label, on which a serial number was marked.

The Inspector picked up the telephone.

'Hello? ... Has Mortimer-Levingston come in? ... No? ... And no one has asked for room 17? ... Hello? ... Yes. ... A parcel from a man's shop on the Grands Boulevards? No need to send that up.'

He rang off and asked in a surly voice:

'Where is Anna Gorskin?'

He felt he was getting somewhere at last.

'Look for yourself. ...'

'In other words she isn't here. ... But she has been here. ... She brought this suitcase, and a letter. ...'

With a rapid movement, Pietr pushed down the fragments of burnt paper, so that nothing remained except ashes.

The Superintendent realized that this was not the moment to take chances; he was on the right lines, but the least slip would rob him of his advantage.

From force of habit he stood up and moved closer to the fire – so abruptly that Pietr jumped and made as though to defend himself. He broke off the gesture, flushing as he realized his mistake.

For Maigret only planted himself with his back to the fire. He was smoking his pipe in short, thick puffs.

Silence now reigned, so long and so full of implications that it jarred on the nerves.

Pietr was on tenterhooks, but determined to keep his countenance. As a retort to Maigret's pipe, he lit a cigar.

The Superintendent began to pace up and down. He leant on the little table that held the telephone, almost shattering it with his weight.

The other man did not notice that he had pressed the bell without lifting the receiver. The result was instantaneous. The telephone rang. A voice from the office inquired:

'Hello? . . . Did you call?'

'Hello? . . . Yes. . . . What did you say?'

'Hello? . . . This is the manager's office. . . .'

Maigret went on imperturbably:

'Hello? . . . Yes. . . . Mortimer-Levingston? Thank you. . . . I'll see him presently. . . .'

'Hello? Hello?'

He had scarcely rung off when the ring came again. The manager's voice asked urgently:

'What is going on? I don't understand!'

'Blast!' thundered Maigret.

He looked searchingly at Pietr, whose pallor had increased and who, at least for a second, was obviously tempted to bolt for the door.

'That was nothing,' Maigret told him. 'Only Mortimer-Levingston coming back. I had asked them to let me know.'

He saw beads of sweat on the other man's brow.

'We were speaking of the suitcase and the letter that came with it. . . . Anna Gorskin. . . .'

'Anna does not come into this.'

'Excuse me. . . . I thought. . . . Wasn't the letter from her?'

'Listen. . . .'

Pietr was trembling. It was obvious. And he was unusually tense. His face, his whole body, jerked and twitched.

'Listen!'

'I'm listening,' said Maigret shortly, still with his back to the fire.

He had slipped his hand into his hip-pocket.

He needed only a second to take aim. He was smiling, but behind his smile could be sensed a concentration strained to the utmost limit.

'Well? I tell you I'm listening. . . .'

But Pietr seized a bottle of whisky, muttering through his teeth:

'All right, then!'

And he poured himself a full glass, swallowed it at one draught, and stood looking at the Superintendent with Fédor Yurovich's glassy stare, a drop of spirit gleaming on his chin.

CHAPTER 12

## *The Two Pietrs*

MAIGRET had never witnessed such lightning intoxication. True, he had never before seen a man swallow a whole tumblerful of whisky at one gulp, refill it, empty it again, fill it for the third time, shake the bottle, and drink the neat spirits to the last drop.

The effect was alarming. Pietr the Lett flushed crimson; a moment later the blood drained from his face, but scarlet blotches were left on his cheeks. His lips turned pale. He clutched at the table, tottered a few steps, then articulated with drunken insouciance:

'You asked for it, didn't you?'

And he broke into a strange laugh that expressed an infinity of emotions – fear, irony, bitterness, perhaps desperation. Trying to prop himself on a chair, he knocked it over. Wiping his damp forehead, he resumed:

'You know, you wouldn't have brought it off all on your own. . . . It's just luck. . . .'

Maigret did not stir. He felt so embarrassed that he almost put an end to the scene by making the other man swallow or inhale an antidote.

He was witnessing the same transformation as in the morning, but ten times, a hundred times more drastic.

Just now he had been dealing with a man in complete control of himself, a man whose keen intelligence was backed by exceptional will-power. A man of the world, possessing wide culture and the most polished manners.

And all at once there was nothing left but a bundle of nerves, a puppet whose strings had gone haywire, a livid grimacing countenance that centred in a pair of glaucous eyes.

The man was laughing! But amidst his laughter and his aimless gesticulations he was straining his ears, bending

94

forward as though listening for some sound beneath his feet.

And underneath was the Mortimer-Levingstons' suite.

'It was well planned,' he said in an unnaturally hoarse voice. 'And you wouldn't have been able to see through it! Sheer luck, I tell you, or rather, a run of lucky chances.'

He bumped into the wall and stayed there, leaning in a twisted position. His features contorted – for this self-induced drunkenness, which was almost a form of poisoning, must have given him a headache.

'Come on. . . . Try to tell me, while there's still time, which Pietr I am. . . . You think Pietr's just a clown, don't you?'

It was repulsive yet pathetic, comic and yet horrible. And the man's galloping intoxication was growing worse with every second.

'It's funny that they haven't come! . . . But they will. . . . And then. . . . Hurry up! . . . Guess! Which Pietr am I?'

His attitude suddenly changed, he clutched his head in his hands and an expression of physical suffering came over his face.

'You'll never understand. . . . The story of the two Pietrs. . . . It's a bit like the story of Cain and Abel. . . . You're a Catholic, I suppose. . . . In my country we're Protestants, and we live with the Bible. But it's no use. . . . I'm certain Cain was an innocent, trusting kind of chap, whereas that fellow Abel . . .'

Footsteps sounded in the corridor. The door opened.

Even Maigret was so startled that he had to bite harder on the stem of his pipe.

For it was Mortimer-Levingston that came in, fur-coated, with the jovial face of a man who has just dined well in good company.

A slight aroma of liqueurs and cigar-smoke hovered round him.

The moment he stepped into the sitting-room his face changed. The colour left it. Maigret noticed an irregularity of feature which was hard to define but which gave something disturbing to his appearance.

One could feel that he had arrived from out of doors; a little fresh air was still caught in the folds of his clothes.

The scene was being played from two directions at once. Maigret could not see it all.

He chose to watch Pietr, who, having recovered from his first shock, was now trying to rally his wits. But it was too late. The dose had been too strong. Realizing this himself, he was desperately straining his will-power to the limit.

His features twisted. He must be peering at people and objects through a distorting fog. When he let go of the table he stumbled, but miraculously recovered his balance, after heeling over at a perilous angle.

'My dear Mor —' he began.

But he met the Superintendent's eye, and continued with a change of tone:

'Oh, all right! All . . .'

The door banged. Footsteps were heard, hurrying away. It was Mortimer-Levingston beating a retreat. At the same moment, Pietr dropped into a chair.

Maigret reached the door with one bound. Before rushing out, he paused and listened.

But it was no longer possible to distinguish the American's footsteps among all the varied sounds in the hotel.

'I tell you, you asked for it!' stammered Pietr, and went on muttering thickly, in an unknown language.

Maigret locked the door, hurried along the passage, and ran down a staircase.

He reached the first floor just in time to intercept a woman who was running away. He noticed a smell of gunpowder.

With his left hand he clutched the woman by her clothes. His right came down heavily on her wrist, and a revolver fell to the floor. In falling it went off, and the bullet shattered a pane of glass in the lift.

The woman struggled. She was unusually strong. The Superintendent, unable to subdue her by any other means, twisted her wrist, and she fell on her knees, screeching:

'Coward!'

The hotel was beginning to stir. Unusual noises were

echoing through all the corridors, emerging from every nook and cranny.

The first person to appear was a chambermaid in a black and white uniform. She raised her hands to heaven and fled in error.

'Keep still!' ordered Maigret, addressing his captive, not the maid.

Both women stopped moving.

'Mercy! I haven't done anything!' cried the chambermaid.

After that, the chaos got worse and worse. People appeared from all sides. In one group the manager was waving his arms. In another there were women in evening dress; and an appalling din was rising from the whole scene.

Maigret decided to bend down and slip handcuffs on his prisoner, who was none other than Anna Gorskin. She resisted. In the struggle her dress tore, and she was reduced to her usual state of half-nakedness, but looking magnificent, with her flashing eyes and curling lips.

'Mortimer-Levingston's room?' Maigret called to the manager.

But the manager was completely out of his depth. And Maigret was all alone among the jostling, panic-stricken crowd, where to make matters worse the women were all screaming, weeping, or stampeding.

The American's suite was only a few yards away. The superintendent had no need to open the door; it was wide open already. On the floor lay a bleeding body, still moving.

Maigret now ran back to the floor above, banged on the door he had locked with his own hand, heard not a sound, turned the key.

Pietr the Lett's rooms were empty!

The suitcase was still on the floor, near the fireplace, with the cheap suit thrown across it.

Cold air was blowing in through the open window, which gave on to a yard scarcely bigger than a chimney.

Below were the dark rectangular shapes of three doorways.

Maigret walked heavily downstairs again, and saw that the crowd had grown calmer. A doctor had been found among the hotel guests. But the women – and the men, for that matter – were taking little notice of Mortimer-Levingston, or of the doctor bending over him.

All eyes were turned on Anna Gorskin, who had collapsed in the corridor, her wrists shackled by the handcuffs, her face furious, and was hurling insults and threats at the spectators.

Her hat had slipped off, and greasy black locks of hair were dangling over her face.

One of the hotel interpreters came out of the lift with the broken pane; with him was a uniformed policeman.

'Clear the place,' Maigret ordered.

He heard vague sounds of protest behind his back. He loomed so large that he seemed to fill the corridor.

Ponderous and implacable, he walked across to Mortimer-Levingston's body.

'Well?'

The doctor was a German who spoke very little French; he launched into a lengthy explanation in a mixture of the two languages.

The lower part of Mortimer-Levingston's face had literally vanished, leaving nothing but a great red and blackish wound.

But the mouth opened, a mouth which was not quite a mouth any more, and a babbling sound emerged, with a gush of blood.

No one understood, neither Maigret, nor the doctor – who was later discovered to be a professor of Bonn University – nor the two or three people who were standing close by.

Mortimer-Levingston's fur coat was spattered with cigar ash. One of his hands lay open, with the fingers spread wide.

'Dead?' asked the Superintendent.

The doctor shook his head, and both of them fell silent.

The uproar in the passage was dying away. The policeman was pushing back the excited crowd, a step at a time, despite all resistance.

Mortimer-Levingston's lips closed, then parted again. The doctor knelt motionless for a few seconds.

Then he stood up and said, as though relieved of a heavy burden:

'Dead, *ja*. It was difficult . . .'

Someone had trodden on the edge of the fur coat, which bore the clear print of a boot.

The police officer, in his silver-braided uniform, had been standing silently for a moment in the open doorway.

'What shall I? . . .'

'Get rid of everyone. The lot,' commanded Maigret.

'The woman is screaming . . . .'

'Let her scream.'

And he went and planted himself in front of the fireplace, which had no fire in it.

# CHAPTER 13

# The Ugala Corporation

EVERY race has its own smell, loathed by other races. Superintendent Maigret had opened the window and was smoking steadily, but faint odours were still making him feel queasy.

Was the Hôtel du Roi de Sicile impregnated with them? Or the street? The smell had first met his nostrils when the black-capped hotel-keeper opened his little window a crack. And it had thickened as he climbed the stairs.

In Anna Gorskin's room you could cut it with a knife. There was food lying all over the place, for one thing. Flaccid sausages of a repulsive shade of pink, thickly speckled with garlic. A plate with some fried fish floating in a sour liquid.

Butts of Russian cigarettes. Dregs of tea in half a dozen cups.

And sheets and underwear that seemed to be still damp, the sourness of a bedroom that was never aired.

It was in the mattress, which he had unstitched, that Maigret found the little grey linen bag.

Photographs and a certificate tumbled out of it.

One of the photos showed a steep, cobbled street, lined with old houses, step-gabled in the Dutch manner, but whitewashed. The black lines of windows, doors, and ledges stood out sharply against the harsh whiteness of the walls.

The house in the foreground bore an inscription in letters that had something of both Gothic and Russian script about them:

6 RÜTSEP
MAX JOHANNSON
TAILOR

It was a big house. A beam jutting from the gable carried a

ulley, used in the old days to hoist sacks of corn up to the
oft. A flight of six steps, with an iron handrail, led from
he street to the front door.

On these steps was a family group, clustered round a short,
greying, colourless man of about forty – the tailor, no doubt –
with a solemn, aloof expression.

His wife, in a satin dress strained to bursting-point, was
seated in a carved wooden chair. She was smiling genially at
he camera, though her lips were slightly compressed, so as to
ook 'genteel'.

In front of them were two children, holding hands. Two
oys, six or eight years old, dressed in knickerbockers that
ame below their knees, black stockings, and white sailor
hirts with embroidered collars and cuffs.

The same age! The same height! The same striking re-
emblance to the tailor.

But there was no mistaking the difference of character
etween them.

One wore a determined expression, and stared at the camera
ggressively, with a kind of defiance.

The other was looking stealthily at his brother. Looking at
im trustfully, admiringly.

The photographer's name was stamped at the bottom:
*. Akel, Pskov.*

The second photograph was larger and even more enlight-
ning. It had been taken at a public dinner. Three long tables,
oaded with plates and bottles, stood at right-angles to the
amera. In the background, on a grey wall, hung a banner
howing six flags, a coat of arms bearing a device of which
he details were indistinguishable, two crossed swords, and a
unting-horn.

The diners were students, eighteen to twenty years old.
They wore caps with narrow peaks edged in silver and velvet
rowns, doubtless of the livid green shade so popular with the
Germans and their Northern neighbours.

The young men had close-cropped hair and, in most cases,
trongly marked features.

Some of them were grinning broadly at the camera. Others

were holding up curiously shaped carved wooden beer-mugs.
A few had shut their eyes, dazzled by the flashlight.

Prominently displayed on the middle table was a slate on
which was written:

UGALA CORPORATION

TARTU

It was one of those students' associations which exist in
every university in the world.

Erect in front of the banner was a young man who stood
out from all the others.

For one thing he was bare-headed, with a shaven crown that
threw his features into strong emphasis.

And while most of his companions were in ordinary clothes,
he wore a dinner-jacket – in which he looked slightly gawky,
for his shoulders were not yet broad enough for it. Across
his white waistcoat hung a broad ribbon, like that of the
highest class of the Legion of Honour.

These were the presidential insignia.

Strangely enough, although most of the guests were looking towards the camera, the shyer ones, by some instinct, kept
their eyes on their young leader.

And the one who was gazing at him the most intently was
his double, seated at his side and craning his neck so as not to
lose sight of him.

The student with the beribboned chest and the student who
was devouring him with his eyes were, beyond question, the
same as the two little boys outside the house at Pskov, the
sons of Johannson the tailor.

The certificate was inscribed in Latin on vellum, in imitation of an ancient document. With a lavish use of archaic
terms, it proclaimed a certain Hans Johannson, student of
philosophy, to be a Companion of the Ugala Corporation.

And the document was signed: *Pietr Johannson, Grand Master
of the Corporation*.

The linen bag also contained a packet tied with string in which

102

there were more photographs and some letters written in Russian.

The photographs bore the name of a firm at Vilna. One of them showed a Jewish woman about fifty years of age, stout, sour-faced, and festooned with pearls like a statue in a church.

Her resemblance to Anna Gorskin was evident at a glance. And one of the other photographs showed Anna herself, at the age of sixteen or so, wearing an ermine-trimmed hat.

The heading on all the letters was the same, in three languages:

EPHRAIM GORSKIN
WHOLESALE FURRIER
FINE SIBERIAN SKINS A SPECIALITY
VILNA – WARSAW

Maigret was unable to read the writing below. But he noticed that one phrase, which recurred in several of the letters, was heavily underlined.

He put these papers into his pocket and to satisfy his conscience made a final tour of the room.

It had been occupied by the same person for so long that it had lost its impersonal, hotel-bedroom atmosphere.

The story of Anna Gorskin could be read in every trifling object, in the stains on the wallpaper, and even on the linen.

Hairs were scattered all over the place – coarse, greasy, black hairs.

Hundreds of cigarette ends. Biscuits in tins and broken biscuits on the floor. A jar of preserved ginger. A big tin containing the remains of a preserved goose, a Polish brand. A pot of caviar, vodka, whisky. A little pot which proved, when Maigret sniffed it, to contain a remnant of unprocessed opium, in compressed wafers.

Half an hour later, back at the Préfecture, he was having the letters translated to him. Certain passages caught his attention:

   *... Your mother's legs are getting more and more swollen. ...*
   *... Your mother asks whether your ankles still swell when you do*

a lot of walking; she thinks you may have the same trouble as she
has. . . .

. . . We are not too much worried, although the question of Vilna is
not settled. We are caught between the Lithuanians and the Poles. . . .
But they both hate the Jews. . . .

. . . Will you inquire about Monsieur Levassor, 65 rue d'Haute-
ville: he has ordered some skins from me, but gives no banker's
reference. . . .

. . . When you have finished your studies you must get married and
come into the business with your husband. Your mother is no help to
me at all nowadays. . . .

. . . Your mother sits all day in her chair. . . . Her temper is
becoming impossible. . . . You ought to come home. . . .

Goldstein's son, who got here a fortnight ago, says your name is
not down at the Sorbonne. I told him that was a lie, and . . .

Your mother has had to be tapped for dropsy. . . .

. . . You have been seen in Paris in the wrong sort of company. I
wish to have an explanation. . . .

. . . I have had some more unsatisfactory information about you.
As soon as business permits, I shall come to see for myself. . . .

. . . If it were not that your mother refuses to be left alone, and the
doctor says there is no hope for her, I would come and fetch you at
once. . . .

I order you to return.

. . . I am sending you five hundred zloty for your train-fare. . . .

. . . If you are not back in a month's time, I shall curse you. . . .

Then more about the mother's legs. Then an account of the
girl's life in Paris, as told by a Jewish student on his return to
Vilna.

Unless you come home immediately, all is over between us.

And a final letter.

How have you been managing for the last year, now I have
stopped sending you money? Your mother is very unhappy. And she
blames me for all that has happened.

Superintendent Maigret did not laugh once. He put the papers in his drawer, locked it, wrote several telegrams, and then made his way to the detention cells.

Anna Gorskin had spent the night in the common lock-up. But Maigret had afterwards given orders for her to be put in a separate cell.

He began by opening the spy-hole. Anna Gorskin was sitting on a stool. She did not start, but turned her head slowly towards the door and glared disdainfully at her visitor.

He went in, and watched her for some time without a word. He knew it would be no use fencing with her, putting the kind of indirect questions that sometimes extract an involuntary confession.

She was too cool-headed to be caught in that kind of trap, and he would only lose face by attempting it.

So he merely growled:

'Will you confess?'

'Nothing!'

'You still deny you killed Mortimer-Levingston?'

'I deny it.'

'You deny that you bought that grey suit for your accomplice?'

'I deny it.'

'You deny sending it up to his room at the Majestic, with a letter in which you informed him you were going to kill Mortimer-Levingston and told him where to meet you outside?'

'I deny it.'

'What were you doing at the Majestic?'

'I was looking for Mrs Goldstein's room.'

'There is nobody of that name staying at the hotel.'

'I did not know that.'

'And why did I find you running away with a gun in your hand?'

'In the first-floor passage I saw a man shoot another and then drop his gun. I picked it up for fear he would shoot me too. I was running to warn the staff.'

'You had never seen Mortimer-Levingston before?'

'No.'

'But he went to the Roi de Sicile.'

'There are sixty people living in the hotel.'

'You don't know Pietr the Lett, or Oppenheim, either?'

'No.'

'That doesn't make sense.'

'I should worry.'

'We shall find the shopkeeper who sold you the grey suit.'

'Bring him along.'

'I have informed your father, at Vilna.'

At this she started, for the first time. But in a flash she jeered:

'If you want him to come here, send him the train-fare. Otherwise . . .'

Maigret kept his temper, watching her with a curiosity not entirely devoid of sympathy. For she had guts.

At first sight her evidence did not hold water. The facts seemed to speak for themselves.

But it is precisely in such circumstances that the police more often than not, find themselves unable to refute the defendant's denials with conclusive evidence.

And in this case there was none! The revolver was not known to the Paris gunsmiths. So there was nothing to prove that it belonged to Anna Gorskin.

What about her presence at the Majestic when the crime was committed? But people can wander about in a large hotel as freely as they can in the street. She claimed to have been looking for someone? That was not necessarily impossible.

Nobody had seen her fire the shot. Nothing remained of the letter that Pietr the Lett had burnt.

Circumstantial evidence? There was any amount of that. But juries will not convict on circumstantial evidence, they mistrust even the most conclusive proof, in their dread of committing a miscarriage of justice – the bogy always conjured up by the defence.

Maigret played his last card:

'I have a report that Pietr is at Fécamp.'

This time he got a reaction. Anna Gorskin jumped. But telling herself that he was lying, she recovered her calm, and retorted nonchalantly:

'So what?'

'An anonymous letter, which is now being checked, says he is hiding in a house belonging to a man called Swaan.'

Her dark eyes, as she looked up at him, were grave, almost tragic.

Maigret, glancing absent-mindedly at Anna's ankles, saw that as her mother had feared she was dropsical.

Her scanty hair was dishevelled and her scalp showed through it. Her black dress was dirty.

And her upper lip showed distinct signs of a moustache.

All the same, she was beautiful, in a vulgar, animal way. Her eyes still fixed on the Superintendent, her lips curled in scorn, her body slightly drawn back, or rather crouched down, instinctively sensing danger, she snarled:

'If you know all that, why ask me questions?'

Then her eyes flashed and she went on, with an insulting laugh:

'Unless you are afraid of compromising *her*! That's it, isn't it? ... Ha! It doesn't matter about me. A foreigner. A tart, going down the drain in the ghetto. ... But as for her, well ...'

Carried away by passion, she was about to break her silence. Maigret, feeling she might be put off by his concentrated attention, assumed an air of indifference and turned his head aside.

'Well – nothing! You hear me!' she screamed. 'Get out! Let me alone! Nothing, I tell you! Not a thing!'

And she flung herself on the ground, with a movement that could not have been anticipated, even by someone with experience of such women.

A fit of hysterics! Her features were distorted. She lay writhing, great shudders convulsing her body.

Only a moment ago she had been beautiful; now she was hideous. She was pulling out her hair in handfuls, regardless of the pain.

Maigret was not disconcerted. He had seen this kind of thing a hundred times before. He picked up the water-jug from the floor. It was empty.

He called a warder.

'Fill this quickly.'

Soon afterwards he was splashing cold water straight into Anna's face. She gasped, her lips parted eagerly, she looked at him without recognition, and at last fell into a stupor.

Even then, a superficial tremor passed over her from time to time.

Maigret lowered the bed, which, in accordance with regulations, was tilted against the wall, straightened the wafer-thin mattress, and with an effort lifted Anna on to it.

He did all this without a shade of resentment, with a gentleness of which he might have been thought incapable. He pulled down the unfortunate woman's skirt over her knees, felt her pulse, and stood at the bedside for a long time, looking at her.

Seen thus, she had the worn features of a woman of thirty-five. Her forehead in particular was lined with slight wrinkles that were not usually visible.

But her hands were pretty and graceful – plump, the nails smeared with cheap varnish.

Maigret filled himself a pipe, prodding it slowly and lightly with his forefinger, like a man uncertain what to do next. For a few moments he strode about the cell, the door of which was still ajar.

Suddenly he wheeled round in astonishment, doubting his own ears.

The blanket had just been pulled up over Anna Gorskin's head. All that could now be seen of her was a shapeless lump beneath the ugly grey covering.

And the lump was moving, shaken by spasms. Listening hard, he became aware of stifled sobs.

Maigret went out quietly, shut the door behind him and walked past the warder. After ten paces, however, he came back, and rapped out in a surly tone:

'Have her meals brought in from the Restaurant Dauphine.'

# CHAPTER 14

# Two Telegrams

MAIGRET read them aloud to Coméliau, the examining magistrate, who seemed worried.

The first was Mrs Mortimer-Levingston's reply to the telegram informing her that her husband had been murdered.

*Berlin. Hôtel Modern. Sick, high fever, unable travel Stop Stones will do necessary.*

Maigret smiled sourly.

'You understand? On the other hand, here is a telegram from the Wilhelmstrasse. It's in *polcod*, so I'll translate it.'

*Mrs Mortimer-Levingston arrived by air staying Hôtel Modern Berlin where she received telegram Paris on returning from theatre Stop Went to bed and sent for American doctor Pelgrad Stop Doctor claims right to professional secrecy Stop Should we insist on visit from police doctor Stop Hotel servant noticed no symptoms.*

'As you see, Monsieur Coméliau, the lady has no desire to be questioned by the French police. Not that I am suggesting she was hand-in-glove with her husband. On the contrary, I feel sure he kept her in the dark about ninety-nine per cent of his activities. Mortimer-Levingston was not the man to confide in a woman, and particularly not in his own wife. But the other evening at Pickwick's Bar she certainly gave a message to a professional dancing-partner, who is now being kept on ice at the Medico-Legal Institute. Maybe that was the one time necessity compelled Mortimer-Levingston to make use of her.'

'And who is Stones?' inquired the magistrate.

'Mortimer-Levingston's private secretary. He served as a link between his chief and his different business ventures. When the crime took place he had been in London for a week. Staying at the Victoria Hotel. I took care not to inform him. But I rang up Scotland Yard and asked them to get hold of him. You realize that at the time when the London police got to the Victoria, Mortimer-Levingston's death had not been announced in England, though the Press may have had wind of it. All the same, the bird had flown. Stones left a few minutes before the arrival of the police.'

The magistrate looked gloomily at the pile of letters and telegrams cluttering up his desk.

The death of a multi-millionaire affects the lives of thousands of people. And all Mortimer-Levingston's business associates were alarmed by the fact that he had met a violent end.

'You think we ought to spread the rumour that it was a crime of passion?' Monsieur Coméliau queried dubiously.

'I think it would be wise. If not, you'll start a panic on the Stock Exchange right away, and ruin some perfectly respectable businesses, including several French firms that Mortimer-Levingston had recently pumped money into.'

'Of course. But . . .'

'Wait a minute! The American Ambassador will ask you for evidence. . . . And you haven't got any! Neither have I. . . .'

The magistrate wiped his glasses.

'So? . . .'

'Nothing! . . . I'm expecting news from Dufour, who has been at Fécamp since yesterday. . . . Let Mortimer-Levingston have a handsome funeral. What does it matter anyhow? There'll be speeches, official deputations. . . .'

For the last few minutes the magistrate had been watching Maigret curiously.

'There's something funny about you,' he remarked suddenly.

The Superintendent smiled and said in a confidential tone:

'Morphine.'

'What!'

'Don't worry, I'm not an addict yet. Only an injection in my chest. . . . The doctors want to remove two of my ribs, they say it's absolutely essential. But it'll be an endless business! I shall have to go into a nursing-home and stay there for I don't know how many weeks. . . . I asked them for two or three days' respite. At worst it seems I shall only lose a third rib. Two more than Adam. But now you're making a tragedy of it, like everyone else. . . . That shows you haven't argued it out with Professor Cochet, the man who's rummaged about inside practically all the high and mighty in the world. . . . He'd tell you, as he told me, that thousands of people get along with all kinds of bits and pieces missing.

'The Prime Minister of Czechoslovakia, for instance. . . . Cochet removed one of his kidneys. . . . I saw it. . . . He showed me lungs, stomachs, all sorts of things. . . . And their owners are going about their business all over the world.'

He looked at his watch and growled below his breath:

'That chap Dufour . . .'

His face resumed its gravity. The magistrate's office was hazy with the smoke from his pipe. Maigret seemed quite at home there, sitting on a corner of the desk.

'I think I'd do better to get down to Fécamp myself,' he remarked at last with a sigh. 'There's a train in an hour.'

'Nasty business,' Monsieur Coméliau concluded, pushing aside the file.

The Superintendent was lost in contemplation of the clouds of pipe-smoke enveloping him. The spluttering of his pipe was the only sound that disturbed, or rather punctuated the silence.

'Look at this photo!' he said suddenly.

He was holding out the one taken at Pskov, with the tailor's white-gabled house, the pulley under the eaves, the six steps up to the door, the mother seated, the father self-consciously posing, and the two little boys with their embroidered sailor collars.

'That's in Russia! I had to look it up in the atlas. Near the Baltic. There are several little countries there – Estonia, Latvia, Lithuania. . . . Encircled by Poland and Russia. The frontiers haven't managed to coincide with the races. The language changes from one village to the next, in some districts. And there are the Jews as well, scattered everywhere, but a people set apart, all the same. Not to mention the communists. There's fighting along the frontiers. There are ultra-nationalist armies. . . . The people live off the fir-trees in the forests. The poor are poorer than elsewhere. Some of them die of cold and hunger. . . .

'Some of the intelligentsia are in favour of German culture, others prefer Slav culture, and others want local traditions and the old dialects. . . .

'Some of the peasants look like Lapps or Kalmuks, some are hulking, fair-haired chaps, and then there's a whole mass of Jews and part-Jews, who eat garlic and slaughter their livestock differently from the rest. . . .'

Maigret took back the photograph from the magistrate, who had glanced at it without much interest.

'Quaint kids,' was his only comment.

Handing him the photo again, the Superintendent asked:

'Could you say which of them I'm looking for?'

There was still three quarters of an hour before the train left. Monsieur Coméliau looked at each boy in turn – the one who seemed to be defying the camera, and his brother, looking away from it as though seeking his advice.

'Photographs like that are terribly revealing,' Maigret went on. 'One wonders how those chaps' parents and teachers can have failed to guess at a glance what lay ahead of them.

'Take a good look at the father. . . . He was killed in a riot, one evening when street fighting broke out between the nationalists and the communists. . . . He didn't belong to either side. . . . He had just gone out to buy bread. . . . I got that piece of information by sheer accident from the proprietor of the Roi de Sicile, who comes from Pskov. . . .

'The mother is still alive, and living in that house. On Sundays she wears national costume, with a tall cap with ear-flaps. . . .

'The children . . .'

He broke off.

'Mortimer-Levingston,' he began again, with a change of tone, 'was born on a farm in Ohio and began his career selling bootlaces in San Francisco. Anna Gorskin was born at Odessa and brought up at Vilna. Mrs Mortimer-Levingston's parents

vere Scots, who emigrated to Florida when she was still a
child.

'And they all assemble here in Paris, a stone's throw from
Notre-Dame. . . . As for my own father, he was a gamekeeper
on one of the oldest estates in the Loire valley.'

He glanced again at the time, and then pointed to the boy in
the photograph who was gazing with admiration at his
brother.

'And now I must go and lay my hands on that lad.'

He knocked out his pipe into the coal-scuttle and just
stopped himself from automatically refilling the stove.

A few moments later Monsieur Coméliau, polishing his
gold-rimmed spectacles, observed to his clerk:

'Don't you find Maigret rather changed? He seemed to
me . . . how can I put it . . . a little on edge . . . a little . . .'

After searching in vain for the right word, he broke off
with:

'What the devil are all these foreigners doing in France?'

Then, seizing the Mortimer file, he began to dictate:

'*The year one thousand nine hundred* . . .'

Inspector Dufour was standing at the same corner where
Maigret had waited, on a recent stormy morning, for the man
in the trench-coat to come out. This was for the good reason
that there was no other bend in the entire length of the steep
lane which, after serving as a path to the few villas on the
cliff-side, dwindled to a mere track and finally petered out in
the close-cropped grass.

Dufour was dressed in black leggings, a short, half-belted
overcoat, and a sailor's cap, such as everyone wears at Fécamp;
he must have bought them as soon as he arrived.

'Well?' asked Maigret, coming up to him in the dark.

'Everything's going fine, Chief.'

The Superintendent found this somewhat alarming.

'What's going fine?'

'The man hasn't gone in, or come out. . . . If he got to
Fécamp before I did, and went into that house, he must be
there still.'

E

'Tell me exactly what has happened.'

'Yesterday morning, nothing. The maid went to do th
shopping. In the evening I arranged for Inspector Bornier t
relieve me. No one went in or came out during the night. A
ten o'clock the lights went off. . . .'

'And then?'

'This morning I took over again, while Bornier went to g
some sleep. . . . He'll be coming along to replace me. . . . Th
maid went out shopping about nine o'clock, the same a
yesterday. . . . The lady of the house went out half an hou
ago. . . . She'll soon be coming home. . . . I suppose she's gor
to pay a call.'

Maigret said nothing. He was well aware of the inadequac
of this supervision. But how many men would it take to keep
really strict watch?

Merely to guard the villa, three would be none too man
And there ought to be one inspector tailing the servant an
another following 'the lady of the house', as Dufour calle
her.

'It's half an hour since she went out?'

'Yes. . . . Hello, here comes Bornier. . . . I'm due for a mea
I've had nothing all day except a sandwich, and my feet a
frozen.'

'Off you go.'

Bornier was a very young man, just starting in the Flyin
Squad.

'I met Madame Swaan,' he said.

'Where? When?'

'On the quay. Just a minute ago. . . . She was going toward
the lower jetty.'

'All alone?'

'All alone. . . . I almost followed her. Then I said to myse
that Dufour would be waiting for me. . . . The jetty is a dea
end, so she can't go far.'

'How was she dressed?'

'In a dark coat. . . . I didn't specially notice.'

'Shall I go now?' asked Dufour.

'I told you to already.'

'If anything turns up you'll let me know, won't you? All you have to do is ring the hotel doorbell three times running.'

This was too silly! Maigret scarcely heard him. Saying to Bornier: 'Stay there!' he suddenly walked up to the gate of the villa 'Swaan and tugged so hard at the bell that he nearly pulled it out. He could see a light on the ground floor, in what he knew to be the dining-room.

He waited five minutes, but nobody appeared, so he climbed the wall – a low one – strode up to the door, and banged on it with his fist.

'Who is there?' a frightened voice quavered from inside; and the children began screaming.

'Police! Open the door!'

Hesitation. Scuffling footsteps.

'Hurry up!'

The corridor was in darkness. As he went in, Maigret could just make out the white patch of the maid's apron.

'Madame Swaan?'

At that moment a door opened and he saw the little girl he had noticed on his previous visit.

The servant did not move. She had her back to the wall and one could feel she was rigid with fright.

'Who did you meet this morning?'

'I promise you, Inspector . . .'

She burst into tears.

'I swear I . . .'

'Monsieur Swaan?'

'No. . . . I. . . . It was . . . Madame's . . . brother-in-law. . . . He gave me a letter for her. . . .'

'Where was he?'

'Outside the butcher's. . . . He was waiting for me. . . .'

'Had he asked you to do anything like that before?'

'No. . . . Never. . . . I never saw him outside this house.'

'Do you know where he asked Madame Swaan to meet him?'

'I don't know anything. . . . Madame was upset all day. She

asked me questions, too. .... She wanted to know how he looked. I told her the truth – that he looked like a man who's going to do something dreadful. When he came up to me I felt frightened, truly I did.'

Maigret suddenly walked out, leaving the front door open.

# CHAPTER 15

# The Man on the Rock

INSPECTOR BORNIER, new to his job, was considerably startled when his superior went past him at a run, brushing by without a word while the door of the villa still stood open.

Twice he called out:

'Superintendent! . . . Superintendent!'

But Maigret never looked round. He did not slow down until a few minutes later he came out into the Étretat road, where there were a few people about. Here he turned to the right, splashing through the mud on the quay, and began running again as he made for the lower jetty.

He had not gone a hundred yards when he saw the outline of a woman. He changed direction in order to pass closer to her. A trawler was unloading, and a lantern hung in the shrouds.

He stopped to give the woman time to reach the circle of light, and saw that it was Madame Swaan. Her face was convulsed, wild-eyed, and she was hurrying along with an unsteady gait, as though picking her way through muddy pools and avoiding them only by a miracle.

The Superintendent was just about to go up to her, and even took a few steps in her direction. But ahead of him he glimpsed the deserted jetty, a long black line stretching into the night with waves splashing up on either side.

It was in that direction that he hurried on. Once past the trawler there was not a soul to be seen. The red and green lights of the channel shone through the darkness. The lighthouse perched on the rocks flashed its beacon at fifteen-second intervals over a wide patch of sea and lit up the nearer cliff-face, lending it, for that brief instant, a kind of ghostly life.

Maigret bumped into some bollards and found himself on

the jetty, which was built on piles, surrounded by crashing waves.

His eyes searched the darkness. He could hear a boat hooting to be let out of the lock.

In front of him was the dark tumult of the sea. Behind him, the town, with its shops and its slippery cobbles.

He walked on quickly, pausing now and then to gaze round with growing apprehension.

Not knowing the lie of the land, he went out of his way in trying to take a short cut. The jetty led him to the foot of a semaphore showing three black balls, which he counted without being aware of it.

Farther on, he leant over the railing, looking down at the great patches of white foam that swirled between the rocks.

His hat blew away. He chased it, but was too late to prevent it from falling into the sea.

Seagulls were uttering piercing cries above his head, and occasionally a white wing flashed against the sky.

Had Madame Swaan found nobody at the meeting-place? Had her companion had time to get away? Was he dead?

Maigret was consumed with impatience, convinced that he would have his answer in a matter of seconds.

He reached the green light and circled round the iron girders that supported it.

Nobody there! And the waves rolled in, one by one, to attack the breakwater – rearing up, tottering, retreating in a great whitish trough, only to return with fresh impetus.

An occasional sound of pebbles grinding against one another. The dim outline of the empty casino.

Maigret was looking for a man!

Turning back, he scrambled down to the beach, among stones that looked, in the darkness, like monstrous potatoes.

He was on a level with the waves now, and their spray blew into his face.

It was then he noticed that the tide was out and the jetty surrounded by a ring of black rocks, with water dashing up and bubbling round them.

It was a miracle that he noticed the man at all. At the first glance he took him for some inanimate object, a vague shadow among shadows.

He looked harder. It was on the farthest rock, where the waves reared their crests most proudly before crashing over in a cloud of spray.

There was something living there. . . .

To reach it, Maigret had to thread his way between the piles supporting the jetty along which he had been walking a few minutes earlier.

The stones were covered with seaweed. His feet slipped. He could hear a surging murmur made up of many sounds – like the scampering of hundreds of crabs, the bursting of bubbles or of sea-grown berries, and the imperceptible quivering of the mussels that coated the lower halves of the baulks on which the jetty rested.

Once, Maigret lost his footing, and one leg sank up to the knee in a pool of water.

He could not see the man any longer, but he was going in the right direction.

The man must have come out here when the tide was lower, for the Superintendent was suddenly halted by a pool two yards across. He groped for the bottom of it with his right foot and nearly fell forward. In the end he had to swing himself over by the crossbeams.

It was one of those occasions when a man prefers to have nobody watching him. He made uncoordinated movements. He constantly missed his mark, like a clumsy acrobat. But he went on, just by sheer momentum. He fell; he picked himself up again. He floundered, undignified and ungraceful.

He cut his cheek, and could never say afterwards whether he had done it in falling flat on the rocks, or scraped it on a nail projecting from one of the beams.

He had another glimpse of the man – hardly believing his eyes because the figure was so still and looked so like one of those stones which, from a distance, resemble human shapes.

After a certain point, the water was lapping round his

shins. He was no seaman. Without realizing it, he began to quicken his pace. At last he reached the group of rocks where the man was perched. Maigret was three feet above him and ten or fifteen paces away.

It did not occur to him to take out his revolver. He went forward, walking on tiptoe where the ground permitted it, loosening pebbles with a rattle that was drowned by the noise of the tide.

Then, suddenly, without a pause, he leapt on the motion-less figure, caught the man's neck in the crook of his elbow, and pushed him over backwards.

The two nearly slipped down, to be swept away by the extra-powerful wave which broke at that instant. It was pure chance that that did not happen. Made deliberately ten times, the same move might have gone wrong every time.

The man, who had not seen his aggressor, was squirming like an eel. His head was wedged, but his body wriggled with an agility which in these surroundings was almost super-human.

Maigret did not want to choke him. He was only trying to keep him still. He had one foot hooked round the farthest pile of the jetty, and that was holding up the pair of them.

His opponent's resistance was brief. It had been merely a spontaneous, animal reaction.

As soon as he had had time to think – or at any rate as soon as he caught sight of Maigret, whose face was almost touching his own – he stopped moving.

He blinked his eyes to indicate surrender, and as soon as his neck was released he pointed vaguely to the heaving mass of water and faltered in a voice that had not yet recovered its strength:

'Take care . . .'

'Shall we have a talk, Hans Johannson?' said Maigret, digging his fingers into the slippery seaweed.

Later he was to admit that at that precise moment his com-panion could have sent him flying into the water with one kick.

The opportunity lasted for only a second, but Johannson,

crouching beside the first baulk of timber, made no attempt to take advantage of it.

Later, too, Maigret frankly admitted that for a moment he had had to clutch his prisoner's foot, to help himself up the rock.

Then, without a word, the two of them set out on the return journey. The tide was already higher. Not far from the shore they were cut off by the same pool that had delayed the Superintendent on his way out, and which was now deeper.

Pietr stepped into it first, was out of his depth after three yards, splashed, spat, and finally emerged, up to his waist in water.

Maigret threw himself forward. At one moment he shut his eyes, feeling that his body was too heavy to be kept afloat.

The two men came together again, drenched and dripping, on the pebbly beach.

'Did she talk?' asked Pietr in a lifeless voice – a voice which at all events held no echo of what makes a man cling to life.

Maigret could have lied to him. But he preferred to answer: 'She didn't say a word. . . . But I know.'

They could not possibly stay where they were. In that wind their wet clothes were turning into icy bandages. Pietr's teeth began chattering first. In the faint moonlight Maigret saw that his lips were blue.

He had no moustache. This was the anxious face of Fédor Yurovich, the face of the little boy at Pskov, devouring his brother with his eyes. But although those eyes were of the same misty grey, there was now a painful intensity in their expression.

Making a three-quarter turn to the right, the two men could see the cliff, with two or three specks of light shining from it – the villas, including Madame Swaan's.

And when the pencil of light from the lighthouse swept past, they could dimly make out the roof that sheltered her, with her two children and the frightened servant.

'Come,' said Maigret.

'To the police station?'

The voice was resigned, or rather, indifferent.
'No.'


He knew one of the hotels beside the harbour – Chez Léon –
and had noticed one entrance that was only used in the
summer, by the few people who came to Fécamp for seaside
holidays. This door led to a room which in the season was
used to serve fairly expensive meals.

In winter-time the fishermen were quite satisfied to drink
and eat oysters and herrings in the main café.

This was the door that Maigret opened. He walked with his
companion across the dark room and ended up in the kitchen,
where a little maid uttered a cry of astonishment.

'Fetch the boss.'

Without moving from the spot, she shouted:

'Monsieur Léon! ... Monsieur Léon ...'

'A room,' said the Superintendent, when Monsieur Léon
arrived.

'Monsieur Maigret! ... But you're wet ... Have you? ...'

'A room. Quickly!'

'There's no fire in the bedrooms! ... And a hot-water
bottle will never be enough to ...'

'You must have a couple of dressing-gowns?'

'Yes, of course. ... My own ... but ...'

He was three heads shorter than the Superintendent.

'Bring them along!'

They went up a steep staircase with sharp, unexpected
bends in it. The room was clean. Monsieur Léon closed the
shutters and suggested:

'A hot toddy, eh? ... A stiff one!'

'That's it. ... But the dressing-gowns first of all.'

Maigret was beginning to feel ill again, from the cold. The
injured side of his chest felt frozen.

For the next few minutes he and his companion behaved
with the easy informality of soldiers in barracks. They undressed in front of each other. Monsieur Léon opened the
door a crack and slipped his arm inside, with two dressing
gowns draped over it.

'Give me the biggest one,' said the Superintendent.

The Lett compared the two.

Holding one of them out to his companion, he caught sight of the sopping bandage, and his face twitched.

'Is it serious?'

'Two or three ribs to be removed one of these days.'

This was followed by a silence. Monsieur Léon broke it by inquiring from outside:

'Getting on all right?'

'Come in.'

Maigret's dressing-gown scarcely reached his knees, leaving a pair of bulging, hairy calves uncovered.

The Lett, slight and pale, with his fair hair and slender ankles, in this garb had the elegance of an acrobat.

'The toddy will be along at once. I'd better put your things to dry, hadn't I?' said Monsieur Léon. He gathered up the two soggy heaps of clothing, went to the head of the stairs and shouted:

'Well, Henriette? Where's that toddy?'

Then he came back with a caution:

'Don't talk too loud. There's a commercial traveller from Le Havre in the next room, and he has to catch a train at five o'clock tomorrow morning.'

# CHAPTER 16

# The Bottles of Rum

It would perhaps be an exaggeration to suggest that in the course of an inquiry cordial relations often develop between the police and the individual from whom they are trying to obtain a confession.

But unless the criminal is a mere soulless brute, a kind of intimacy nearly always grows up. No doubt owing to the fact that for weeks, sometimes for months, the detective and the offender are concentrating entirely on one another.

The detective is doing his level best to get some idea of the criminal's past life, to reconstruct his ideas and anticipate his slightest reactions.

For both, it is a matter of life and death. And when they come face to face, the situation is sufficiently dramatic to break down the barrier of polite indifference that in ordinary circumstances divides one man from another.

Detectives have been known, after catching a criminal, at the cost of strenuous efforts, to grow attached to him, visit him in jail, and give him moral support till the very moment when he mounts the scaffold.

This partly accounts for the behaviour of the two men once they were alone in the room. The hotel-keeper had brought in a charcoal stove, and a kettle stood singing on it. Close at hand, flanked by two glasses and a sugar basin, stood a tall bottle of rum.

They were both cold. Huddled in their borrowed dressing gowns, they bent over the inadequate stove, which was not enough to warm them.

Their attitude had the casual ease of the guardroom or the barracks, an informality seldom found except among men for whom social conventions have temporarily ceased to count.

Perhaps it was simply because they were cold. Or more

likely because both were suddenly overwhelmed by fatigue.

It was over! No words were needed to convince them of that!

So they dropped into their respective chairs and stretched out their hands towards the kettle, staring vaguely at the blue enamel stove, which formed a kind of bond between them.

It was the Lett who picked up the bottle of rum and, with deft movements, prepared the two glasses of toddy.

After taking a few sips, Maigret asked:

'Did you mean to kill her?'

The reply came at once, with equal simplicity:

'I couldn't do it.'

But the man's whole face was working, contorted by a tic that seemed to give him no respite.

Sometimes he blinked rapidly, several times in succession; sometimes his lips twisted this way or that; sometimes his nostrils quivered.

Pietr's firm, intelligent features were becoming blurred.

The Russian was gaining the upper hand – the tramp with the overstrained nerves, whose movements Maigret did not bother to watch.

Thus he failed to notice that his companion had seized the bottle of rum, filled his glass and emptied it at one gulp, and that his eyes were beginning to glisten.

'Pietr was her husband? . . . He and Olaf Swaan were one and the same person, isn't that so?'

The Lett could not keep still. He got up and looked round for cigarettes; but there were none to be found, which seemed to distress him. As he went past the table where the stove stood, he helped himself to some more rum.

'That's not the place to begin,' he said.

Looking his companion straight in the face, he added:

'You know everything, or practically everything, don't you?'

'The two brothers at Pskov . . . twins, I suppose? You're Hans, the one who looked so admiringly and submissively at the other.'

125

'When we were still quite small, he began to treat me like a servant. . . . Not only when we were by ourselves, but in front of our schoolfriends. . . . He didn't say "servant", he said "slave". . . . He had noticed that I liked it. . . . I *did* like it. I still don't know why. . . . I saw everything through his eyes. . . . I would have died for him. . . . Later on, when . . .'

'Later on, when . . .?'

Twitching features. Blinking. A mouthful of rum.

Then a shrug, as much as to say:

'Oh well. . . .'

And he resumed in a steady voice:

'Later on, when I fell in love with a woman, I don't think my devotion to her was greater. . . . Probably less. I used to fight the other boys if they questioned his leadership. I wasn't as strong as they were, but I felt a kind of exhilaration when they knocked me about.'

'You often get that sort of bossiness with twins,' observed Maigret as he mixed himself another toddy. 'Excuse me a moment.'

Going to the door, he called to the proprietor to ask for his pipe, which had been carried off with his clothes, and for a packet of tobacco.

'And could I have some cigarettes?' his companion put in.

'And some cigarettes, *patron*. . . . *Gauloises bleues!*'

He sat down again. Both men waited in silence till the maid had brought what they wanted and gone away again.

'You were at Tartu University together . . .' Maigret began again.

The Lett could not sit still. As he smoked he bit into his cigarette, spat out flakes of tobacco, strode jerkily to and fro, picked up a vase that stood on the mantelpiece, put it down in a different place. His words came with feverish haste.

'That's where it began, yes. My brother was the best student of his year. All the professors were interested in him. The other students accepted him as a leader. So much so that although he was one of the youngest, they elected him President of *Ugala*.

'We used to drink a lot of beer in the local taverns. I drank most of all. I don't know why I started drinking at that early age. I had no reason for it. Anyhow, I've been drinking all my life.

'I think it was chiefly because after a few glasses I could begin to imagine a world made to my own measure, where I should play a brilliant part. . . .

'Pietr was very hard on me. He used to call me a "dirty Russian". You don't know what that means! Our mother's mother was Russian. And in our country, especially after the war, the Russians were regarded as lazy, drunken idlers. . . .

'At that time the communists were provoking riots. My brother collected the members of *Ugala*, they went to a barracks and armed themselves, and then they started fighting, right in the middle of the town.

'I was afraid. . . . It wasn't my fault. . . . I was frightened. . . . I couldn't walk. . . . I stayed in a tavern behind closed shutters, and sat there drinking till it was all over. . . .

'I wanted to be a great dramatist, like Chekhov. I knew all his plays by heart. But Pietr laughed and said:

'"You'll never be anything but a wash-out!"

'There was a whole year of disturbances and riots, with life completely disrupted. The army wasn't strong enough to keep order, so the civilians formed themselves into armed bands, to defend the town.

'As leader of the *Ugala* boys, my brother became a person of importance, taken seriously even by the most respectable citizens. Before his moustache began to grow he was being tipped as a future statesman in an independent Estonia.

'But order was restored, and then a scandal came to light and had to be hushed up. When the accounts were drawn up it turned out that Pietr had used *Ugala* chiefly for his own ends.

'He was a member of several committees, and he'd been cooking the books of all of them.

'He had to leave the country. . . . He went to Berlin, and wrote to me to join him there.

'That's where we both started our careers.'

Maigret was watching the other man's over-excited face.

'Who did the forgeries?'

'Pietr taught me to imitate every kind of writing, and sent me to study chemistry. I lived in one small room and he gave me 200 marks a month. . . . A few weeks later he bought himself a car to take his mistresses for drives. . . .

'Mostly, we used to touch up cheques. . . . Pietr would give me a ten-mark cheque, I would alter it to ten thousand marks, and he would get cash for it – in Switzerland or Holland; once even in Spain. . . .

'I used to drink a great deal. He despised me and ill-treated me. Once I nearly got him caught, unintentionally, because of a forgery that wasn't quite as good as the others.

'He thrashed me with a walking-stick. . . .

'And I didn't say a word! I still admired him. . . . I don't know why. . . . But everybody was impressed by him. . . . There was a time when, if he'd wanted to, he might have married the daughter of a German cabinet minister. . . .

'Because of that bungled cheque we had to move to France; at first I lived in the rue de l'École-de-Médecine. . . .

'Pietr wasn't working alone any more. He had joined up with several international gangs. . . . He was travelling abroad a lot, and making less and less use of me. . . . Only now and again, for forgeries, because I had got very handy at that job. . . .

'He used to give me a little money.

'"Drinking is all you'll ever be fit for, you dirty Russian!" he kept saying.

'One day he told me he was going to America on some terrific job that would make him the equivalent of a multi-millionaire. He ordered me to move to the country, because the Paris police had already questioned me several times.

'"All I want is for you to keep quiet! That's not too much to ask, is it?"

'At the same time he ordered me to find him a whole batch of false passports, and I did.

'Then I went to Le Havre. . . .'

'And there you met the future Madame Swaan.... Her name was Berthe.'

A silence. The other man's Adam's apple swelled in his throat.

At last he broke out:

'How I longed to become *something*, then! She was the receptionist at the hotel where I was staying.... She used to see me coming back drunk every night.... And she scolded me....

'She was very young, but serious. She made me think of a home, and children....

'One evening when she was telling me off and I wasn't too hopelessly tight, I wept in her arms, and I believe I promised to mend my ways.

'And I think I'd have kept my word. I was fed up with everything! Sick of dragging around....

'It lasted nearly a month. ... Silly, when you come to think of it. ... On Sundays we used to go and listen to the band in the public gardens. ... It was autumn. ... We'd walk back by the harbour and look at the boats....

'We didn't talk about love.... She said she was my friend.... But I knew that one day....

'Oh yes! ... One day, my brother came back.... He needed me in a hurry.... He had a whole suitcase full of cheques to be doctored.... Heaven knows how he'd collected so many! They were drawn on every big bank in the world....

'On this occasion he'd turned himself into an officer of the merchant navy, by the name of Olaf Swaan....

'He took a room at my hotel.... For weeks on end, while I was doctoring the cheques – for that's a delicate job! – he went round all the ports along that coast, looking for boats to buy....

'His new scheme was going well. He told me he had concluded an arrangement with one of the biggest American tycoons – who wasn't to appear openly in the business, of course.

'They were trying to bring all the most important international gangs under one leadership.

'The bootleggers had already reached agreement. . . . Now they needed small boats to smuggle the drink. . . .

'Do I need to tell you the rest? Pietr had cut off my supply of alcohol, so as to force me to work. . . . I was shut up in my room all day, surrounded by watchmaker's eyeglasses, bottles of acid, pens, inks of all kinds, and even a portable printing-press. . . .

'One day I went into my brother's room without warning.

'Berthe was in his arms. . . .'

He grabbed the bottle, which was down to its dregs by now, and emptied it at one draught.

'I left,' he concluded, in a voice that sounded strange. 'It was all I could do. I left. . . . I caught a train. I trailed round all the *bistros* in Paris for days and days. . . . I ended up in the rue du Roi de Sicile, dead drunk and as sick as a dog!'

# CHAPTER 17

## Hans and His Mistress

'IT seems to be my fate to be pitied by women. When I came round, Anna was fussing over me. . . .

'And she took it into her head to stop me drinking, too! . . . She treated me like a child, the same as Berthe used to do! . . .'

He laughed. His eyes were misty. It was exhausting to watch his restless movements and the play of his features.

'But she stuck to it. As for Pietr . . . Well, I suppose it's not for nothing that we're twins; we must have *some* things in common.

'I told you he could have married a German girl from one of the best families. . . . But no! He married Berthe, a little later, when she had left her job and gone to work at Fécamp. . . . He didn't tell her the truth.

'I can understand it all. . . . The need to have a decent, quiet corner somewhere, you know. . . .

'He has children! . . .'

This seemed to be too much! The man's voice broke. Real tears came into his eyes; but they dried at once, as though his eyelids had scorched them up.

'Until this very morning she still believed she'd married a real captain in the merchant navy. . . .

'He came now and then to stay with her and the kids – it might be for a couple of days, or for a month. . . .

'Meantime, I couldn't get rid of the other one. . . . Anna. . . .

'Heaven alone knows why she loved me. . . . But she did, that's certain. . . .

'And I treated her the way I'd been treated all my life by my brother. . . . I used to insult her. . . . I was always humiliating her. . . .

'When I got tight she used to cry. . . . And I used to drink on purpose! . . .

'I even took opium and all kinds of filth. . . . On purpose! . . .

'Then I fell ill, and she nursed me for weeks. . . . Because this broke down in the end. . . .' He pointed at his body with an air of disgust. Then he said imploringly:

'Won't you ask for some drink?'

After only a second's hesitation, Maigret went to the head of the stairs and called:

'Send up some more rum!'

The Lett did not thank him.

'From time to time I would run away to Fécamp, to hang about the villa where Berthe had gone to live. . . . I can see her now, pushing her first baby in its pram. . . .

'Pietr had been forced to tell her I was his brother, because of the resemblance. . . .

'One day I had another idea. . . . Way back, when we were kids, I used to imitate Pietr's manner, out of admiration for him. . . .

'Now I was tormented by so many strange ideas that one day I dressed up like him and went to Fécamp. . . .

'The servant had no suspicion. . . . But as I was about to go in, the little girl appeared, and called:

'"Papa! . . ."

'I'm a fool! I ran away! But the idea was fixed in my mind. . . .

'At rare intervals Pietr used to send word for me to meet him. . . . He needed something forged. . . .

'And I'd do it! Why?

'I hated him, and yet I was still under his thumb. . . .

'He was dealing in millions, staying in big hotels, appearing in society. . . .

'Twice he was caught, and both times he got away with it. . . .

'I never concerned myself with his organization, but you'll have guessed the kind of set-up, as I did. So long as he was on his own, or with only a handful of accomplices, he'd kept to moderate-sized affairs. . . .

'But he caught the attention of Mortimer-Levingston,

whom I never met till the other day. . . . My brother had brains, daring, one might even say genius. Mortimer-Levingston had the veneer of respectability and a well-established international reputation. . . .

'Pietr's job was to rope in the big sharks, under his leadership, and organize the deals.

'Mortimer-Levingston acted as their banker. . . .

'All that meant nothing to me. . . . As my brother had predicted, when I was only a student at Tartu, I was a washout. . . . And like all washouts, I was drinking, alternating between bouts of depression and excitement. . . .

'I had just one lifeline. I still wonder why I clung to it through all that buffeting. I suppose because it was associated with my only glimpse of possible happiness: Berthe. . . .

'As ill-luck would have it, I went down there last month. . . . Berthe gave me advice. . . . And she added:

'"Why don't you follow your brother's example?"

'Then I was suddenly struck by an idea. I couldn't understand why I hadn't thought of it sooner. . . .

'I could actually become Pietr, whenever I chose!

'A few days later he wrote to say he was coming to France and would be needing me.

'I went to Brussels to wait for him. I got into the train on the wrong side and hid behind a pile of suitcases until I saw him get up to go to the toilet. I was there first. . . .

'I killed him! I'd just swallowed a whole bottle of Belgian gin. The hardest part of it was getting him undressed and into my own clothes. . . .'

He drank greedily, with an eagerness Maigret would not have thought possible.

'When you first spoke to Mortimer-Levingston, at the Majestic, did he notice anything?'

'I rather think so. But only as a vague suspicion. At that time I had only one idea – to see Berthe again. . . .

'I wanted to tell her the truth. . . . I felt no real remorse, and yet I couldn't take advantage of my crime. . . . In Pietr's trunk there were all sorts of clothes. . . . I dressed up like a tramp, in my usual style. I left the hotel by the back way.... I felt Mortimer-Levingston was following me, and it took me two hours to shake him off....

'Then I hired a car and had myself driven to Fécamp....

'Berthe couldn't understand why I'd come.... And once I was in front of her, and she was asking me questions, I no longer had the courage to confess!

'You arrived on the scene.... I saw you from the window.... I told Berthe the police were after me for theft, and asked her to save me.

'After you left, she said:

'"And now, go! You are dishonouring your brother's house...."

'Yes, she really said that! And I left! And we went back to Paris, you and I....

'There I found Anna.... A scene, of course! Tears!... At midnight, Mortimer-Levingston arrived. By this time he'd understood everything, and threatened to have me killed unless I took Pietr's place once and for all....

'It was a very serious matter for him.... Pietr was his only contact with the gangs.... Without him, he had no hold over them....

'Back to the Majestic.... And you after me!... I heard some talk about a detective being killed.... I saw you, all stiff inside your jacket....

'You'll never know how sick I was of life....

'At the idea that I was doomed to act the part of my brother for the rest of my days....

'You remember the little bar?... And the photo you dropped?...

'When Mortimer-Levingston came to the Roi de Sicile, Anna had objected.... She felt the arrangement was to her disadvantage.... She realized that my new role would take me away from her....

'That evening, in my room at the Majestic, I found a parcel and a letter....'

'An off-the-peg grey suit and a note from Anna to say she

was going to kill Mortimer-Levingston, and appointing a place for you to meet her. . . .'

The atmosphere was now thick with smoke, and warmer. The outlines of things were becoming hazy. . . .

'You came here to kill Berthe,' said Maigret deliberately.

His companion was drinking. He emptied his glass before he replied, clutching the mantelpiece to keep himself upright.

'To put an end to everything! Including myself! . . . I was sick of it all! . . . I had one idea left, of the kind my brother used to call typically Russian. . . . That Berthe and I should die together, in each other's arms. . . .'

He broke off, to say in a changed voice:

'Idiotic! It takes a quart of spirits to give one an idea like that. . . . There was a policeman outside the gate. . . . I was sober by then. . . . I wandered about. . . . This morning I gave the maid a note asking my sister-in-law to meet me on the lower jetty, and telling her that unless she brought me a little money herself, I should be caught. . . .

'Revolting, wasn't it? . . .

'She came. . . .'


Then, propping his elbows on the marble chimney-piece, he suddenly burst into tears – not like a man, but like a child. In a voice half choked by sobs, he continued his story.

'I hadn't the courage. . . . It was almost dark. . . . The sea was roaring. . . . And her face – with the first signs of anxiety. . . . I told her everything. . . . Everything! Including the murder! . . . Yes, with the change of clothes in the cramped space in the toilet. . . . Then, because she looked as though she were out of her mind, I swore it wasn't true. . . . Wait! Not about the crime. . . . But about Pietr being a scoundrel. . . . I shouted at her that I'd made that up, to revenge myself. . . . I expect she believed me. . . . *One always believes things like that.* . . . She dropped her bag on the ground, with the money she had brought. And she said . . . No. She couldn't speak.'

Raising his head, he turned his tortured face towards Maigret and tried to take a step forward – but staggered and had to clutch at the mantelpiece.

'Pass me the bottle, you. . . .'

And in the 'you' there was a note of gruff affection.

'Here. Give me that photo a minute. . . . You know . . .'

Maigret produced Berthe's photograph from his pocket. This was his only mistake throughout the whole business – the mistake of imagining that at that moment it was she who was foremost in Hans's thoughts.

'No. . . . The other. . . .'

The one of the two little boys with sailor collars.

The Lett gazed at it as though in a trance. The Superintendent was looking at it upside down, but he could see the admiration with which the fairer boy was watching his brother.

'They took away my gun with my clothes,' Hans suddenly said in a flat, colourless voice, as he looked round him.

Maigret's face was scarlet. He pointed awkwardly to the bed, where his own revolver lay.

At that the Lett relaxed his grip on the chimney-piece. He was not staggering now. He had mustered all his strength.

He walked past, within a yard of the Superintendent. They were both in dressing-gowns. They had shared the bottles of rum.

Their two chairs were still facing each other on either side of the charcoal stove.

Their eyes met. Maigret had not the heart to turn his head away. He was expecting a pause.

But Hans went by, very erect, and sat down on the edge of the bed; the springs creaked.

The second bottle had a little rum left in it. The Superintendent picked it up. It clinked against his glass as he poured.

He drank slowly. Or rather he pretended to drink. He was holding his breath.

At last came a report. He drained his glass at one gulp.

In official language, the story ran:

*On – November 19 – , at 10 p.m., Hans Johansson, born at Pskov, Russia, of Estonian nationality, no occupation, resident in the rue du Roi de Sicile, Paris, having confessed to the murder of his*

*brother, Pietr Johannson, killed in the North Star express on —
November of the same year, took his own life by shooting himself in
the mouth, shortly after being arrested, at Fécamp, by Superintendent
Maigret of No. 1 Flying Squad.*

*The projectile, of 6 mm. calibre, passed through the roof of the
mouth and lodged in the brain. Death was instantaneous.*

*The body was transported, for the necessary formalities, to the
Medico-Legal Institute, which delivered a receipt for it.*

CHAPTER 18

# *The Wounded Man*

THE ambulance men left, though not until they had enjoyed
glass of Madame Maigret's own plum brandy – she prepared i
every year in her native village in Alsace, where she always re
turned for the summer holidays.

When the door had closed behind them and the sound c
their footsteps was dying away down the stairs, she went int
the bedroom, where the wallpaper was patterned wit
bunches of roses.

Maigret, looking a little tired, with narrow dark ring
round his eyes, lay in the big bed whose most prominen
feature was a red silk eiderdown.

'Did they hurt you?' asked his wife, as she tidied the room

'Not too badly. . . .'

'Are you allowed to eat?'

'A little. . . .'

'Fancy you being operated on by the surgeon who's don
all those kings, and people like Clemenceau and Cour
teline. . . .'

She opened the window to shake out a rug on which one c
the ambulance men had left footmarks. Then she went into th
kitchen, shifted a saucepan on the stove, took off the lid, an
put it on again slightly to one side.

'Tell me, dear . . .' she began when she came back.

'What?'

'Do *you* believe that business about a crime of passion?'

'Who are you talking about?'

'About that Anna Gorskin, whose trial opens today, th
woman who lived in the rue du Roi de Sicile and says she wa
in love with Mortimer-Levingston and killed him out c
jealousy.'

'Oh, so it's today?'

'It doesn't make sense.'

'Well, you know, life is so complicated.... You might pull my pillow up.'

'You think she'll be acquitted?'

'A lot of those women are!'

'That's just what I'm saying.... Wasn't she mixed up in your case?'

'Vaguely....' he sighed.

Madame Maigret shrugged her shoulders. 'It's a lot of use being married to a member of the Judicial Police!'

But she said this with a smile.

'When anything happens,' she added, 'I hear about it from the concierge.... She has a nephew who's a journalist....'

This time Maigret laughed too.

Before his operation he had gone twice to see Anna in the women's prison.

The first time she had scratched his face.

The second time she had given him information which had led to the arrest, on the following day, at a lodging-house in the Bagnolet district, of Pepito Moretto, the murderer of Torrence and of José Latourie.

Days and days without news! From time to time a telephone call from the ends of the earth, which did little to reassure her. And then, one fine morning, Maigret had come home, looking completely done up, collapsed into his chair, and gasped:

'Go and fetch the doctor....'

Now she was bustling happily about the flat, pretending to grumble, just for the principle of the thing; stirring the stew that bubbled in her saucepan, carrying buckets of water here and there, opening windows and shutting them again, and from time to time inquiring:

'A pipe?'

On the last occasion there was no reply.

Maigret was asleep, the lower half of his body buried under the red eiderdown, his head sunk into the big, soft pillow, his features in repose, while all these homely sounds fluttered round him.

In the Palais de Justice, Anna Gorskin was fighting for her life.

Pepito Moretto, in the Santé prison, knew that his was doomed. In the cell where he was kept under permanent observation, he prowled ceaselessly round and round beneath the gloomy eye of a gaoler, whose face was divided into squares by the grating in the door.

At Pskov, an old woman in national costume, the flaps of her bonnet pulled down over her cheeks, would now be on the way to church, her sledge gliding over the snow while a drunken coachman lashed at a pony which trotted jerkily, like a clockwork toy.

# MORE ABOUT PENGUINS
## AND PELICANS

*Penguinews*, which appears every month, contains details of all the new books issued by Penguins as they are published. From time to time it is supplemented by *Penguins in Print*, which is our complete list of almost 5,000 titles.

A specimen copy of *Penguinews* will be sent to you free on request. Please write to Dept EP, Penguin Books Ltd, Harmondsworth, Middlesex, for your copy.

*In the U.S.A.*: For a complete list of books available from Penguins in the United States write to Dept CS, Penguin Books, 625 Madison Avenue, New York, New York 10022.

*In Canada*: For a complete list of books available from Penguins in Canada write to Penguin Books Canada Ltd, 41 Steelcase Road West, Markham, Ontario.

MARGERY ALLINGHAM

# POLICE AT THE FUNERAL

Starring Albert Campion, bland, blue-eyed, deceptively
vague professional adventurer, and Great Aunt Caroline,
that formidable and exquisite old lady, ruling an ancient
household heavy with evil.

Uncle Andrew is dead, shot through the head. Cousin
George, the black sheep, is skulking round corners. Aunt
Julia is poisoned, Uncle William attacked. And terror
invades an old Cambridge residence.

*Also published*

MYSTERY MILE

SWEET DANGER

THE TIGER IN THE SMOKE

THE CRIME AT BLACK DUDLEY

MR CAMPION AND OTHERS

MORE WORK FOR THE UNDERTAKER

TRAITOR'S PURSE

# SIMENON IN PENGUINS

'The best living detective-writer ... Maigret is the very bloodhound of heaven' – C. Day Lewis in a broadcast